Breasting the Waves

Breasting the Waves

On writing and healing

Joanne Arnott

PRESS GANG PUBLISHERS

VANCOUVER

First Edition 1995

The Publisher acknowledges financial assistance from the Canada Council, the Book Publishing Industry Development Program of the Department of Canadian Heritage, and the Cultural Services Branch of the Province of British Columbia.

Some of these writings have previously appeared in *By, For & About: Feminist Cultural Politics* (Women's Press, 1994); *Miscegenation Blues: Voices of Mixed Race Women* (Sister Vision Press, 1994); *Wiles of Girlhood* (Press Gang Publishers, 1991); *(f.)Lip, Open Letter, Contemporary Verse II, Room of One's Own* and *absinthe.*

The author would like to acknowledge the support of the Canada Council in financing her tour of southeastern Australia, July–August, 1994, for which some of this writing was developed.

This is a collection of nonfiction writings. Some names and details have been changed. One piece, as discussed in the introduction, reaches beyond verifiable truth in some elements, yet remains substantially true in its details. Please note that irregularities in word usage, grammar and spelling represent intentional choices by the author.

CANADIAN CATALOGUING IN PUBLICATION DATA

Arnott, Joanne, 1960–
    Breasting the waves

    ISBN 0-88974-049-6

    1. Self-actualization (Psychology). 2. Healing. 3. Adult child abuse victims. 4. Métis. I. Title.
BF637.S4A76 1995   158´.1   C95-910663-4

Edited by Lenore Keeshig-Tobias
Copy edited by Nancy Pollak
Cover and text design by Val Speidel
Front cover photograph © 1995 Brian Campbell
Typeset in Monotype Garamond
Printed and bound in Canada by Best Book Manufacturers
Printed on acid-free paper ∞

Press Gang Publishers
101-225 East 17TH Avenue
Vancouver, B.C. V5V 1A6 Canada

for my partner, Brian

and for our children,

Stuart

Harper

Theo

. . .

and for barbara findlay

Contents

Acknowledgements

Thanks to the Creater.

Thanks to the land:

1960   Winnipeg, Manitoba

1967   Vancouver, British Columbia

1972   Rural Manitoba

1976   Windsor, Ontario

1979   Small town, Manitoba

1980   Windsor, Ontario

1982   Vancouver, British Columbia

1991   Taipei, Taiwan

1992   Steveston, British Columbia

1995   Vancouver, British Columbia

Thanks to truth-telling women, including the late Audre Lorde, in particular for her essay, "Uses of the Erotic: The Erotic As Power"; to Maria Campbell, for *Halfbreed*; to Beth Brant for *A Gathering of Spirit*; to Sally Morgan, for *My Place*; to Lillian Allen, for "The Birth Poem."

Thanks to my partner, Brian Campbell, for over a decade of family-making, life-sharing, and love. Thanks to our families, including all our sisters and brothers, mothers and fathers, the in-laws and the outlaws, nieces and nephews. Thanks to Barb Kuhne, Val Speidel, Della McCreary and Shamina Senaratne—Press Gang Publishers—for ongoing friendliness and support. Thanks to Beth Brant, barb findlay, Sharon Lee, Alma Lee, Smaro Kamboureli, Lynnette D'anna, Ann Decter and Angela Hryniuk, among others, for your various contributions to this writer's life. Thanks to Nicholas Zenthoefer, Phil Hall, John Ditsky, Peter Stevens and The Ugly House poets. Thanks to Nym Hughes and Sarah Davidson, Nancy McRitchie, Bonnie Fabian, Celeste George, and the many women and men I met through AWARE. Thanks to Sandy Oliver. Thanks to Don Smith and Stewart Steinhauer. Thanks to Sheila Sherban, I miss you. Thanks to the women and men of the downtown eastside co-op, which held many happier times than those recorded here. Thanks to my midwives Camille Bush, Mary Sullivan and Gloria Lemay. Thanks to Lawrence Redwood, Pat Forrest and the healing circle participants, and to the medicines.

Thanks to the participants in Beth Brant's fiction class, at WestWord V, for accepting the essay "Double-Take" as my response to Beth's assignment, "Write something sexy."

"The Country-Born" was written to assist me in digesting certain aspects of Unlearning Racism theory, and to explore *my place,* as well as to elucidate and teach; thanks in particular to Flo Robertson, Sarah Lyons and Don Smith for reading and responding.

Thanks to the participants in Andreas Schroeder's creative nonfiction class, UBC, for energetic responses to "Wild Girls: A Resurrection" and "Last Year's Corpse." The latter reads much more clearly as a result, and although in the end

I did not restructure "Resurrection," as advised, hopefully its weaknesses are lessened by proximity to other related essays and stories. "Wild Girls: A Resurrection" is an exploration, personal fragments connected in with larger historical and societal patterns; I do not intend to imply in any way that sexual abuses and societal denial are unique to my situation, racially or geographically.

Thanks to Lenore Keeshig-Tobias, Beth Brant and others for assistance in the endless reworking of "A Trip in the Autumn." Thanks, Lenore, for your editorial support and for the title "Surrendering a Solitary God."

I would like to acknowledge the great gift of teaching, love and support I have received from the lesbian and Two-Spirited people in my life.

In memory of Albert O'Neil and Jake Klassen.

Healing Circle

. . . came to the healing circle. Thought it would be women only, and was wrong. Some smile warmly, some hold separate, some look as unhappy as I am.

Tumbled into the safety of a darkened room, candlelit and cleansed with smudge. Heard strong prayers of welcome and orientation, words that pulled my walls and doors apart . . . Creater . . . Mother Earth . . . Grandmothers . . . Grandfathers . . . Four Directions . . .

Crystal the size of a young fist begins a slow migration of the circle, as each person sets down "what I have in my heart."

I have come with a new friend, and later an old friend walks in, and still later, we find that we newcomers have borrowed her pillow, her blanket, to seat ourselves upon, this first time.

Over the months as we speak from our hearts, the stories unwind to overflow the textbooks, the newspapers, the minds of anthropologists and criminologists everywhere. All of the issues are raised, not in the abstract, but carried out on waves of grief or rage, cleansed with the medicines, and grounded in the shape and structure of the healing circle.

Opening ourselves to the nourishing energies of Mother Earth and the Creater, we sit close to one another's stories, and offer ourselves to each other as warmth, caring, sharing, human bodies, enspirited and alive.

Many blessings.

In January 1995, I travelled to Maple Creek, Saskatchewan, to co-facilitate an Unlearning Racism workshop with my good friend, the prominent gay rights activist and lawyer barbara findlay. We'd been looking forward to this workshop for some time. We were to be working with the trainees for a new Aboriginal Healing Lodge, one of several new regional institutions set up by the federal government to replace the archaic and cruel Prison for Women (P4W) in Kingston, Ontario. Ignorant of the ways of bus companies, we found ourselves at Maple Creek Junction, a good five miles from our destination. I stood enjoying the fresh air, the snow, and a long-awaited cigarette, while barbara went into the truck-stop to investigate our further travel options.

Dropping my cigarette in the snow, I walked into the station. My attention was immediately taken by a small white poster with sketches of two Aboriginal women, taped to the counter. I approached. The remains of these two young women had been found in the country outside one of Saskatchewan's larger centres. The women's ages were estimated to be between nineteen and twenty-one. The times of their deaths were estimated to be about two years prior to the time their bodies were found.

A kind of cold, quite separate from the prairie winter, invaded me.

In the late summer of 1982, I took a bus from Vancouver, where I'd been visiting family, to Windsor, Ontario, where I was living and going to school. The fact that I got on that bus at all must be seen as a measure of my willpower, because all of my soft body cried out to stay with my family, to live in this new world of women's community and west coast. But, rationally, I was only a year away from completing my degree and, rationally, I was not in any actual danger in Windsor, Ontario. It is true that all my nourishing friendships had ended, all my family had moved away from Windsor, and I was, as I joked at the time, *drowning in mainstream*. Still, a year is not such a very long time and the mature thing to do is to complete what you've begun, finish what you've started.

On the bus I met a man some fifteen years older than me. He sat behind me, weaving tales of life in the North for anyone who would listen. Dreaming of the North is a common thing for southern Canadians, and I had it bad. The dream of endless expanses and a simpler life, something somehow more true than what I had right now. With that bait on the hook, he caught me. Over the hours of travel across prairie, we talked about the possibility of me living and working in Rae Lake, a place where he said he lived and I had never heard of. He left the bus in Thunder Bay.

I arrived in Windsor, grim but determined, and arranged rooms for myself, registered for classes. The professors went out on strike, and Bill arrived to persuade me to go North with him now. The fact that most of my self was clearly opposed to what I was forcing myself to do, to finish my schooling, made it very easy for him. My friends tried to dissuade me, but without the regular round of school and without any relationship untroubled and powerful enough to provide me with an anchor, it was not difficult to allow myself to be cajoled into leaving, to come back to finish this project, *university,* some other time.

Before I'd left Vancouver, my sister Ani had approached me with worry, saying she'd had her tarot cards read and the reader had told her, *one of your sisters will have a brush with death, but there is nothing you can do about it. It is a result of how she chooses to live her life.* We spent an hour together that afternoon, speculating about our sisters. A case could be made for each one—insecure housing, violent relationships, drug or alcohol abuse: it could be any one. It didn't occur to either of us that it might be me, or at least neither of us said so. The truth is, we make ourselves vulnerable by refusing to listen to the voiced needs of our soft bodies.

Hitchhiking through the autumn allowed me to observe the great beauty of the trees in the northern lakes region of Ontario in that season. I'd hitched across Canada twice in the years previous, with other boyfriends, but always in summer. We stopped, Bill and I, in Manitoba, to visit some of my family. My brother tried very hard to open my eyes to this person I was travelling with. "I've been conned before," he insisted, "and I'm telling you . . ." I was as committed to this new path as I'd been to school, unfortunately, and so we went on.

Sleeping in a field in Saskatchewan, feeling the icy cold reach up through the earth and pull at my body's heat, began to offset that thrill of freedom that comes with abandoning all. One day by the side of a twisting river, I watched a long time as an eagle and a hawk argued above us. Bill had many plans that fell through. He made many phone calls to people who may or may not have existed. On Thanksgiving day, we caught a ride with some young men from the Alexis Reserve in Alberta, and they brought us to the home of Josephine.

We sat up and talked late with Josephine and her young son, sharing tales of our lives. Her son drew a picture for me, and Josephine and I connected really well. She fed us a Thanksgiving feast and made up a bed for us in her living room.

> *you made me a pallet on the floor*
> *oh yes you made me a pallet on the floor*
> *you didn't have to do it but*
> *you opened up your door and you*
> *made me a pallet on the floor*

Megwetch.

Bill and I woke in the morning to see Josephine awake and at work, dressing a moose in the kitchen. "I have so much to tell you," she said.

The further north we got, the more nervous and the less stable Bill became. He began picking fights, twisting the words of my confidences and throwing them back at me in ways that stung. Finally, in the country near Hotchkiss, Alberta, I'd had enough. I walked up a hill at the side of the road, sat down, and told him to get lost.

I hadn't chosen the scene of my battle very well, an innocuous turn in the road with only strands of barbed wire and the late autumn bush visible. He wouldn't *just leave*. We argued, and as I began to best him in the argument, he threatened to break my jaw. Eventually, Bill said we needed to set up camp and *just talk*. It wasn't until he led the way off the road that I realized exactly what kind of danger I was in. For the first time I became aware of the isolation of that place, felt that quailing of the bowels, the heightening senses.

"A Trip in the Autumn," the oldest piece in this collection and the only one that transgresses the loose rules of creative nonfiction, was written in the late fall and early winter of 1982–83, in Vancouver. Bill's interior monologues are based partly in imagination and equally on the loquacious monologues he indulged in while asleep. The story covers only a few intense days, after a series of assaults, ending with departure. But of course, there is always more, as much of a story existing outside of the story as within its bounds.

At one point, for example, Bill showed me a photograph of a young First Nations woman, his "last girlfriend," who he said was dead. Bill's driver's license placed him at home in Reno, Nevada, not in Rae Lake. I like to joke that I was *saved by the middle class,* as the people who assisted me in getting free of Bill were a white, middle-class, nuclear family in a big car.

At the women's shelter in Edmonton, a paid helper, a young woman with cropped blonde hair, a white coat and blue eyes, asked me what I was writing so furiously over the first few days and nights I was there. I let her read the journal I was updating. She looked at me—with my bruised eye and face, bruised neck all the way around—and said, "Pretty bad, *if it happened.*"

I didn't call the RCMP until I was back in Vancouver. Much to my outrage, they refused to even take a statement.

Bill had my family's phone numbers, in Manitoba, and he called them, sometimes as himself, sometimes pretending to be a friend or his own brother trying to find out where I'd gone, threatening my nieces. The RCMP, after repeated complaints from my father and brother, called on me to make a statement. Finally. I did so, fully aware that it was the complaints of the men, and not the endangerment of a woman, that pushed them to action.

At the women's shelter, I saw a young woman whose boyfriend had indeed broken her jaw. The distrust of the young worker was more than countered by the light touch of another young woman, Métis, who invited me to go out with her and her friend. When I declined, she offered to fix my hair. I said yes, and she took her time brushing my hair, combing it out, and binding it into a french braid, the first of my life. My best friend at the shelter was Billy Jack, whom the blonde worker insisted on calling by the more feminine name Billy had used when signing in. Billy Jack was the diplomat, welcoming newcomers with a coffee, offering us a joke to make our troubled lives just a little easier. Billy Jack had another name, which she told me with a mock-grim face and a twinkle. "They call me Indian," she said in a low, mean voice. "Indian."

I walked into the workshop in Maple Creek on a powerful tide of murder-related emotion. I'd been doing some intensive work with healing circle members before leaving the coast, and my emotions were flowing very strongly. As a facilitator, the trick with Unlearning Racism workshops is to be able to move nimbly from head to heart to head again. With my heart at flood, I found it very nearly impossible. With the patience of the participants, and solid support from barbara both day and night, the workshop went well enough.

Arriving again at the truckstop at Maple Creek Junction, barbara and I were more than ready to head home. Used to big city ways of doing things, ignoring what was around us and waiting for someone to tell us what to do, we failed to notice our bus to Regina until it pulled out of the parking lot, onto the highway. A fast conversation with the gas jockey revealed that if we waited for the next bus, we'd miss our flight home. The taxi service had folded. There was no place to rent a car. Pragmatic barbara turned to me finally and said, "We'll just have to hitchhike. I don't see any other option."

The fear, again. The cold unrelated to January in Saskatchewan. I asked her, "Do you carry a gun or a knife?"

At that point, and no doubt in response to my question to barbara, the gas jockey sighed. "If you want to wait 'til I get off shift, I can drive you." Then louder, to the waitress, to whom he was married: "You feel like going for a drive?"

In the Acknowledgements, you will find a long list of thank you's, for debts accrued over the years I worked on the pieces in this collection. It wasn't until after I had submitted a complete draft of the manuscript to publishers that I began to attend the healing circle. There I found the beginning/end/transitional place, the answer to the personal challenge posed in the title story, "Breasting the Waves."

All my relations.

Sensitive

"I really love babies," she said.

"Uh huh," I said, dandling the baby. He was already learning to walk, he was grasping firmly on my fingers and standing, wobbling, a half-step forward, two steps back.

"In fact," she said, "I'm giving birth right now."

This caught my attention. I looked at her directly. She was, indeed, squatting, yet her waist was thin as mine and she was also fully clothed. We were neighbours meeting for the first time, in a small artist's gallery and coffee bar, with sombre artworks hanging from the walls and rising from the floor on wooden pedestals.

I noticed that the guy making café au lait was listening intently, head bowed, watching the three of us through his hair.

"You are?" I said. "Right now?"

"Yes," she said, then looked mildly embarrassed. "I'm making love quite a lot now, because that's how my babies come. Last night I was up 'til one-thirty or so, making love. I feel fine now, though.

"Oh, I cried a bit," she smiled softly. "A little bit sensitive, you know?"

Double-Take: A Poet
Represents Her Poem

Before giving birth and exploring the whole transformative
process of pregnancy and birth, I had a miscarriage and two
abortions. On the occasion of my second abortion I wrote
the poem "Abortion (Like Motherhood) Changes Nothing." The title reflects my mother's opinion of motherhood,
and the hope she passed on to her daughters that non-
motherhood would provide a healthier alternative, for us, to
her experiences as a Roman Catholic, working-class wife
and mother. The first sentence came to me while I was
walking down the street. It is this: "I am a cunt, and the
folds of my face are purple." That is the point of view taken
in the poem. It is a cynical rebuttal of my mother's hopes.

Abortion (like Motherhood) Changes Nothing

I am a cunt, and the folds of my face
are purple. My mouth, delicate and moist,
a pale pink.
Like your tongue, like the roof
of your mouth my throat
arcs gently, while

all around me pulses
my heart (the pump
of power, the vibrant
juices). At the base of my throat
is an organ, the organ
is growing, it swells
from lemon to orange to melon
as the long days pass. Here
at the base of my throat
life and death are meeting
for a hot red time.
Life and death are meeting
at the base of my throat, i do not
scream, i do not
gurgle. Life and death
are cavorting, and when
all is done,
receding,
both of them, all of us,
back down the throat to
the lip of my face,
out into the world
of men—

off to
meander again.
The organ forgotten reduces
to her virgin size; my self
slips back to the usual
uncondensed form;

and my cunt,
she is returned to
a shadowy half-known place,
off along
the tenuous edge
of being.
My face

remembers her eyes, her nose
and ears, her taste buds.
My face
speaks well, again, in places, in that

stilted *human* tongue.

I wrote that in 1985.

Shortly thereafter, I became engaged in another bout with fertility. As I describe the experience in another poem, "Now again I am pregnant/this time with child." While I was exploring this pregnancy process, the women in my family began for the first time to really acknowledge consciously, and to one another, that incest and violent sexual abuse is intrinsic to our shared family experiences. Coming to consciousness individually, and as a group, has required an amazing degree of persistence and has released huge amounts of energy, often as rage. Although I remember only pieces of a life, I know now that I am a sexual abuse survivor.

Turning to this poem again with this revived consciousness, what I hear is a loud, protesting voice from the other side of forgetting, the other side of occlusion, the part of myself who will never hesitate to say precisely *what is.*

Listen again to some of the words:

I am a cunt . . .

. . . my throat
arcs gently, while
all around me pulses
. . . the pump
of power . . .

. . . At the base of my throat
is an organ, the organ
is growing . . .

Life and death are meeting
at the base of my throat . . .
scream . . .
gurgle . . .

Clearly the knowledge bleeding through is that of oral rape.

The rest of the poem portrays the process of occlusion, forgetting, and its consequences. I say we "recede," that the "organ" is "forgotten." I describe the world as one "of men," my movement through it "meandering." I describe my return to my body/senses, to a "usual" though still rather disembodied state of being. The ending is as much about

this second, inner reading as it is about abortion; the awareness of occlusion is plain:

> My face
> speaks well, again, in places, in that

> stilted *human* tongue.

On both levels of this work I damn the agreed-upon
reality, acknowledging the huge chunks of our lives that are
denied place and consciousness within that construction.
The unheard of and denied become literally the unthinkable, no matter how many times we experience them. What
remain are potent gaps in our personal and collective mem-
ories, knots of tension in our bodies and communities, and
free-floating, random images of fear. This experience of
dissonance is, for most of us, fundamental.

All of this poem was written, reworked and revised
without ever tilting the balance of memory/nonmemory,
knowing/not knowing. It took a few more years and the con-
tinued interaction with others before that balance began to
shift.

It is not true that we are individual. In body and mind,
we are endlessly divisible, and we do become divided when
our experiential worlds and the spoken, agreed-upon reality
are consistently incongruent. Nor is it true that we are alone
in this world; isolation is one of the greatest tools used to
disempower people(s), and within the cult of the individual
we as people, as communities, remain fragmented.

We are forged by this culture at the same time that we are

its living tendrils. We create this culture too, consciously and unconsciously, in our best and our worst moments. In acknowledging the splits within ourselves, and between us, by locating the potent gaps and making space for them to materialize—by realizing them—we undermine dissonance. We make sense, for ourselves, for everyone.

She Carries the Poem
That Carries Me

AUGUST 9. *There's a horde of teenagers at the park; I want to go home but I am afraid to go past them. Eventually I duck into a church base-ment to call a taxi. I crumple up my bus transfers —three of them— and throw them away. I'm sitting down relaxing when the man who has an outdoor kiosk, who loaned me his phone, comes in carrying a cardboard box which he drops when he sees me.*

"I thought you were going home, you're not supposed to be in here."

A drunk, stoned teenager walks in and out again, a tall male with long brown hair, striped shirt, jeans. I suddenly realize that I haven't left at all, I'm still in danger. Once I'd got inside I just spaced out, went numb, pretended to be safe or forgot the danger instead of going home, instead of going through the danger to actual safety. I find my transfers and straighten them out.

My brother and my sister appear, they are my helpers. They lead me away. We try to avoid the teenagers; we do see a few, but we're safe. We cut through a park. Because there are dogs on either side, we cut through the middle.

Some years ago I wrote a poem called "in my dance class," a true story about the impact of poverty and shame on the physical body—*my* physical body—how circumscribed social possibilities became limited physical abilities, how social, physical and mental awkwardness reflected back and forth on one another like Indra's pearls. The poem was published in a special issue of *Fireweed*, "The Issue is Class," and went out into the world. An important aspect of "in my dance class" is the ending, the hopefulness of it, in reclaiming my right to be here, a human among human beings. In allowing emotion and trusting others for whole minutes at a time, I saw and shared a possibility for liberation.

A story about this poem came back to me through an acquaintance. She gave me a word-picture of an impoverished friend of hers, standing in a backyard, pulling a copy of my poem from her pants pocket. To show, to share with. In that poem I gave back a bit of her self, and in that word-picture a piece of me was returned also. She carries the poem that carries me. The poem is the vehicle inside of which she and I meet, embrace, and give each other strength for the journey.

AUGUST 10. *I dream about me and my dad arguing. I dream about talking to my junior high school friend about living at home. A little girl who is abandoned/not abandoned. Much of the dream occurs at my early childhood home. I decide and I promise not to mistreat the girl. I help with her science homework.*

That first publication happened around the time I gave birth for the first time. At university I'd had a few things published, done a few readings, but it was easy to discount these as I knew many of the organizers and editors. Although I was unable to recognize it, I was suffering through an intense experience of culture shock. The people I met and knew at university in Ontario were not at all the same as the people I'd known in small-town Manitoba. The regional disparity and class differences I was absorbing without understanding, combined with the confusion of moving out from under the patriarchal rock of my family home, became overwhelming. It took a few years of collapse and retreat, on the west coast, before I was able to sort and digest all the information and emotion I was carrying around. By the time of that first publication and that first birth, I was coming back into society, for the first time knowing who I was and where I stood in relation to the rest.

I have always written, most often from the depths and about them. The publication encouraged me and I kept writing, learning to adapt my writing life, like everything else, to the new reality of being a mother. This shift and adaptation gave me plenty to write about, as I became the bigger one, as I struggled to name my reality as it danced and changed so rapidly, as I watched this new life and had my understanding revised and validated. My suspicion that babies are not evil was confirmed. My vision of the unity of life was upheld, amplified. My sense of the unfitness of this society, its biophobia, became a more specific and detailed critique.

My deepest hopes and wildest fears leapt to the fore, and when I had time, I wrote about it.

Four years later, my trust and support in the world was such that I was able to envision and create a manuscript, a selection of old and new poems that share an itinerant view of girlhood and coming of age, at the same time demonstrating the dynamics of occlusion, denial, remembering. *Wiles of*

Girlhood (Press Gang Publishers, 1991) was woven together through another pregnancy, creative decision-making and prowess bristling all through my life.

AUGUST 11. *I dreamed about my school friend again, I told her that when I was young I was in love with her. I was embarrassed to do so but she looked so sweetly at me; no problem. We looked for a place to be alone together, before she had to go, back to another town, where she lived.*

Over the years since I turned twenty, and particularly since I turned twenty-five, I have come to know myself in a way that is radically different from the way I was raised. The tension between reality as accepted, spoken, given, and that which is perceived and surges from within, seems to be the matrix of my creativity. As I uncover and reclaim all these pieces of reality lost, the writing flows, the tension in my body and mind ebbs, the original Joanne surfaces and inhabits my life for longer and longer periods.

AUGUST 12. *Puberty. Want to run away from home—feel bad about leaving.*

Last December I turned thirty. With support from my partner Brian and my friends Sandy and barb, I had a big birthday party and invited people from all the different compartments of my life—family, diverse friends, women from the Unlearning Racism community, people from the co-op. I wrote a series of poems expressing as many different aspects of myself as I could—the tense and the sad, the silly and the sexy—and I read them at the party. Then I opened my presents. For three days afterward I had a warm good feeling inside, the unloved and doubtful child was just so pleased, so eased, so succoured by that celebration.

Shortly thereafter I received the offer to publish *Wiles of Girlhood*. I accepted, with a glum voice hiding the terror.

AUGUST 13, 14. *Dream about making travel plans. Dream about travelling. Dream about other women I know who are mixed heritage, like me.*

The book is scheduled to come out this fall. That gave me the final impetus to act on my long-standing desire to visit my hometown and family in Manitoba. I told my Vancouver friends that I wanted to go now, before the book came out, because once it did I wasn't sure what my welcome would be. To my family in Manitoba, I said I wanted to come because I hadn't been back for so long; if I waited one more year, it'd be a full decade. So I made my plans and sat back to wait for my income tax and child tax credit to come in the mail. When it came, I left.

JULY 7. *My son and I are standing in front of a large loom for doing beadwork. I am proudly presenting it to him, it is bigger than he is. He is intrigued, a bit confused. It is immense. He says, "My uncle D. gave this to me?" I say, "My uncle D. gave it to you." It's to make a tapestry of his life. Upon waking, I tell the dream to Brian and am horrified—I proudly present my son with the beading/beating of his life, to make his life a tapestry/travesty. Family heirloom.*

I often write from my dreams, from my feelings, from sensations in my body. When I feel stuck, or moved, or troubled, these sensations are like a dense cloud and the writing is like rainmaking. The words precipitate and fall from my hands, and I keep going until the cloud is dissipated, or until exhaustion, or until I really must stop to care for the children. I enjoy all the phases of writing—the purely generative, the revisioning, the selection of work for submissions or presentations. It is not unusual for me to laugh or cry or curse when I am writing.

Sometimes I feel sick to my stomach. Then I need to balance the writing time with talking time, get some outside human support for myself, or support my own humanity by stopping to eat, rest, exercise. Writing essays and other nonfiction comes from a different place in my body, but I try not to simply write from my head. That approach isn't as satisfying as a centred, embodied writing/reading experience.

Preparing to visit Manitoba, the place I left at fifteen and haven't visited since twenty, I started noticing my dreams again, writing them down and thinking about them. I slowly realized this wasn't simply a vacation, or even a last-ditch visit, but a healing journey, a way and a time to gain a renewed sense of resolution about my past, family, and reality, before moving on.

JULY 24. *Wrenched from my body at least two, possibly three times. First the terror, then a kind of pleasure in it—a totally uncontrolled, uncontrollable, huge and terrifying sensation. Something happened and then a huge whirling, wrenching experience, so physical—and then a kind of floating, but in a fast wind.*

There was so much more—lots more information that I needed to write down in order to understand. It was definitely about Manitoba, definitely about responding to physical attack and overpowering in the only way of escape left open—splitting from my body. Splitting is not just a word, it is a terrifying reality.

Something happened. Then my flight, a wrenching and whirling that is in itself terrifying and takes all my attention, then it subsides and happens, detail for detail, again. It is so strong, I cannot see past to what provoked it. Then it subsides and when it happens, detail for detail, for the third time, I'm kind of used to it—the sensation is plea-surable, delicious, as well as, or after, the terror. The dream carried on and provided many more clues, but I haven't retained them. One of the last was "boy scouts"—boy's coat?

All the things I have realized, recognized, recovered, have changed and transformed me. Going to Manitoba is like sliding into the past, a transformed being taking up the space made for someone who is the Joanne of others' memory and making. It is wonderful to see everyone, to visit, to look at and move through that landscape with which I am so intimately familiar. But I don't speak very much. I listen. I observe. I see how oppression lays like an undisturbed blanket of snow across my family and my old prairie home. Oppression, denial, forgetting, disassociating, discounting. The people I know live within it, breathe it, try to make sense of their lives without ever stepping out from under the weight of oppression. They are good people, more or less restricted, more or less confused by, more or less malformed by oppression. On a few occasions I feel very alone, sad about compromise and silence.

JULY 26. *Archeology. A whole raccoon family found at one site. When we find them we get strange names.*

I tell my father this dream. Another time, we talk about having Indian heritage. "Not on my side, as far as I know. Ask your mom." I did, months ago, and she panicked. Not only incest, but ancestors too, tug at the seams of reality and are greeted, banished, feared as if they loom catastrophically.

AUGUST 5. *Indians: "Was it you who told? We thought it might have been you." I shake my head. "No, no, it wasn't me. I would never do something like that."*

A crime has happened, I was a witness or strongly suspected the truth. I didn't see the whole thing, but I came in shortly after and they spoke freely before me. When I left, I phoned right away—the police? Someone else? I told, then pretended that I didn't.

The younger ones, a woman and two men, some elders too are there, in a house or trailer. The second time I go, they ask me if it was me who told. I'm terrified and I lie, pretending it was someone else. But it was me and I leave quickly. I think we're talking about murder and I'm afraid of being killed.

Then I'm at the co-op in the city. Two white women have just painted over the mural. It was not a complete picture, poorly done, of an old man's face—an Indian face. "Did you paint up that mural? I didn't even get a chance to look at it."

Those who paint it over do so without consensus, without permission. They sneak in and paint it all a pale blue before anyone can say anything. They paid off the inexperienced artist before the work was completed. It meant a lot to me. I am heartbroken.

My Grass Cradle is the working title of my second collection. Thematically, it interweaves more about class, race, region, as well as the girl and woman and body and dreams of *Wiles of Girlhood.* It is very much in the gestation phase, and active compilation will have to wait until both inner and outer time agree, until it is ripe and I am ready.

Whatever part writing does/may play in my public life, it is integral to my private self, my being in the world. Through journal-keeping and long, long letters, writing is the practice that returns me to centre and keeps me connected to and communicating with myself and those who are emotionally close, geographically distant. Writing is both how I make things to show and to share, and an everyday and private occupation, how I maintain balance, how I digest things.

The crafting of a poem is a ritual: the casting of a spell of containment to safely send bits of real life out into the world, independent of the human who experienced and wrote them. The writing of a poem is never complete until the spell is effective, until it is able to evoke, express, explore, and end—resolve, banish—the rawness of experience. In reading fragments of poems, the spell is broken and the reader is left unsettled, as the unresolved pieces of life drift through their system. The difference between formal and informal writing is just this structure and promise: informal writing is raw and all over, whereas formal or public writing carries the promise to resolve or at least to anchor, to tie up, most of what is evoked in the writing.

Nonfiction writing is, in some sense, an easier task for me than poetry or fiction, because I am simply sharing what I know, and not striving to name the unnamed/unnameable. This has not always been so. In the past, before I became sure of my audience, I was never able to complete a nonfiction piece. Oppression had taken root and the power of those internalized voices who sang of my worthlessness, my strangeness, my invisibility and the pointlessness of all my endeavours, was persuasive, pervasive. Through the work I have done in Unlearning Racism, the emotional bloodletting, the support for naming and thinking through my fears, and the opportunities to speak live and in person before other human beings, I have come to trust my audience and myself. Knowing I will be heard, there is a point to revision and rewriting. Completion is possible, not something to avoid or idly wish for.

AUGUST 16. *I dream a famous Black actress is going to my hometown. I want to warn her, I am afraid for her, I want to tell her to tone down her style. I also just want to see her, because I admire her. But I am leaving, realize I won't be here when she arrives. Then I'm less anxious, I know it'll be okay. I decide that she can take care of herself.*

The function of oppression is to divide, and to conquer. The victim of oppression (as opposed to the survivor) can be recognized by the depth and width of her or his shame. In *Wiles of Girlhood*, my aim is not to humiliate my family, but to express myself. All of the writings come from my innermost strivings, from the shadow side, a place where I once lived and dwelt much of the time. Today I succeed in living in the present and in daylight. Writing has helped me to do that. I take pride in my writing, pride in myself and in the strengths and successes of my family.

I need to behave in a way that is good for me, I need to conduct myself and my life in a way that is healthy. Hiding in the shadows, or hiding the shadows themselves, is not healthy. In writing as in life, I need to bring the shadow into the daylight, and to celebrate.

Survivor's Manual

Step One

Get safe. Remove yourself from dangerous situations and from all dangerous people except yourself. Include yourself in safe situations and among safe people.

Honour yourself. Put yourself and your healing front and centre in your life. Do not agree to being used abusively by others. Deflect destructive urges away from yourself and use that power to carve out a liveable space, to build a life you want to be at the centre of.

Step Two

Get real. Begin to notice your body, your mind, your feelings, your environment, your connections. Notice what you say, what people say, how we respond or fail to respond to one another. Noticing what's true/real is important, more important than judging. If you find you've just invested an hour of your time in self-persecution, make a note of it, and find something more pleasurable to do. Leave space for feelings. Feeling and expression are the basis of positive change, the keys to healing. Remember your deepest sense of right, and begin again to guide your conduct based on that inner sense, rather than on what is usual, acceptable, normal, or what you can get away with.

Have a passion. Writing, music, dance, drumming, singing, painting, weaving, carving—anything you can do repeatedly that expresses "who I am right now." You can do this as a release for built-up energies, either with others or independently of others. Some of these, like writing and carving, you can collect and build up over time, to reveal how much your efforts change and improve. You can, if you choose to, go public eventually, sharing your truths with the world and very possibly hearing the world say back, "that was very important for me, thank you."

Reclaim your history as a wonderful person, and build on it.

Step Three

Get support. Talk about it: how you feel, what you're thinking about, what happened to you then, how it affects you now, what your hopes and dreams are and were. The ability to erase yourself may have got you through some dangerous situations. The more you get safe, the less useful self-erasure is as a way to relate to the rest of the world, or for discovering and meeting your own needs and desires. Connect with other people who can play the role of witness as you move along the healing path and reconnect with the truths of your life. A web of supportive relationships will help you to help yourself, over and over.

Relate. Make connections in all directions—then with now, you with me, other with self. Take up the tarot, the I Ching, dreamwork, some practice you can compare yourself with and check yourself against, some "universal" perspective. Do simple healing rituals that connect you with others in safe, affirmative, freeing ways: sweats, moon and solstice rituals, healing circles, support groups. Become involved in a community or organization you care about, one with goals or values that reflect your own.

Challenge your comfort zones. If you are usually silent, speak. If you protect yourself with walls built of your own words, be silent, practise listening. Develop dynamic relationships with friends, children, a lover. Take many small risks, becoming your full self, remaining engaged.

STEP FOUR

Get on with it. Survivors of chronic abuse have a whole new world to experience, once you are safe enough in your world and with yourself. Build up your connections with the natural world, with beauty, joy, pleasure and with your own humanity. Survivors of incidents of sudden trauma need to let your worldview be shaken up, too. Reality includes both the best and the worst you can imagine.

As you go along with healing, you will notice the rhythms and recognize the process. You become more skillful in riding the waves, and making the best decisions for yourself, blossoming into the most wholesome person possible. Allow yourself to change and move on, and to revitalize old situations with new energies, possibilities, powers.

These steps are not a staircase, but rather points on the wheel, steps in a spiral. You have visited and/or will visit each one many times at different levels and from new angles. Confusion, unhappiness, despair, rage and flashbacks are part of the healing process. Discovering/rediscovering joy, calm, laughter and vitality are part of it, too.

Eventually you will want to stop changing yourself to try and fit in, and start changing the world to make it a more safe and comfortable place for you and for all of us. At some point you may find yourself turning around that cry from the deep, "I need help!" to the important and deep recognition, "Help needs me," "I am help." It's not a place to hurry toward, but if we honour ourselves, have a passion, and relate, it comes walking out of us eventually.

Storytelling: A Constellation

I'm interested in the 'how' & 'why' of stories, the material circumstances which govern their writing, and the language/s which impede or speed the pen.[1]

how does a coyote girl get a tale outta her mouth?[2]

This contemporary analysis from Canada revisits these questions at the post-colonial crossroads of race, gender, identity and experiment and moves them forward toward a new space for women to write our lives.[3]

If they were to know my life, all their theory would fly out the window.[4]

ONE

Storytelling stands at the edge of the campfire, listening in, part of but not in control of whatever's going on.

In urban settings, Storytelling can be found leaning against a wall, inside at office parties and at the academy, outside of ordinary houses and cultural buildings, in the markets, even in the alleys that run behind bars late at night.

At just the right moment, a low murmur begins, growing to a growl.

In worlds without walls, Storytelling passes through, weaving.

One by one by one each one surrenders their attention to Storytelling. In the quiet focus of energies, Storytelling's voice carries far. In the quiet collection of energies, Storytelling's voice is deeply resounding. The collectivity of our attention throws Storytelling's shadows up high against the trees.

In the suburbs, in the cities, in the farm kitchens, the details vary, but the overall trend of energy and voice, of creation and regeneration through co-operation and choice, is about the same.

There is another woman here, whose even teeth shine with big words that glitter between her careful lips. Her strength is Virgoan, her power is discriminatory, and she expresses her love of the world through strategic analyses. Her work is to look, listen, learn, then wrench apart and reconstitute (language? culture? society?) in a new order. She is very clever. Her spittle is very refined and hard to see, yet each tiny droplet reverberates with meaningful syllables. She calls herself a friend to Storytelling. Secretly, she wants to be Storytelling's new road manager.

This other woman moves from a careful posture, each step is usually well reasoned, though from time to time her passionate discourse sweeps her along, and reason comes after, later, like a broom tidying up her trail. How she came to love Storytelling is a good question. But love her she does. She keeps setting up new situations in which the two can meet. Each encounter is full of surprises for all.

For instance: At a conference this other woman is perched on a log the sea swept in many years before. Storytelling shambles up. Storytelling flops onto the sand beside the log. The two women attempt intercourse, that other woman high on her log and Storytelling down in the mutter.

The impulse to share story happens, and Storytelling begins.

"I am such a slut," says Storytelling.

With a shocked sniff the other woman promptly corrects her. "You mean, you are promiscuous."

Storytelling subsides. "Whatever," she mumbles.

"So. Go on," the other woman begins, attempting to encourage, oblivious to having obviated Storytelling.[5]

The surprise for the audience is how boring and short the story is. For Storytelling, confusion results from being turned on and shut down at the same time. For the other woman, the wild reticence of Storytelling is what intrigues her, the mysteriousness of her responses and her failure to respond in a predictable or acceptable, fashion, manner.

A slut is one who has intercourse or otherwise passionate relations with others, many others, perhaps indiscriminately. That is definitely true of Storytelling. According to this dictionary here,[6] a slut is "A slovenly woman, a slattern," with "slovenly" meaning messy, disorganized, or dirty, and "slatternly" meaning, of course, "sluttish." Storytelling is definitely all of these things, at least some of the time. Leaning against the wall of a church and having a pee at midnight, that kind of thing. Stories woven from a ragtag and unkempt bundle of words, images, feelings, only coming together in a sensible way at the very end of the telling, through the processes of telling, made tidy by full hearing and understanding.

"Promiscuous" seems like a classier version of the same thing, and in the sense of indiscriminate, it is. It does not, however, carry the associations of either woman or dirt, and these are important. Without women and dirt, life cannot go on. "Of mixed and disorderly composition"[7] is the first meaning the dictionary offers, with a strong secondary implication of "casual." These may or may not be relevant, valid. These may or may not be what Storytelling intended to say.

What I love about Storytelling is her juiciness, her shagginess, her ranginess, her unpredictability. She will come through anyone and everyone, at one time or another, boiling to the surface of a person and breaking out, called forth by and erupting into social situations polite or intimate, impolite or impolitic, transforming these situations into human situations for whole long moments.

Too

Lies grow out of fear and truths out of safety. Storytelling can be lies or truths or pieces of both.

Storytelling is a constellation of powers, an alignment of energies, a transitory cohesiveness and integrity of focus and purpose, a force created almost entirely through the act of listening.

Listening is the ground of being upon which stories grow, against which story exists, and out of which Storytelling weaves her particular magic. All voices have access to stories, all beings have access to voices. It is the act of listening that makes story manifest, makes it happen.

Storyteller *is the Keeper of Tales which encompass history, meaning, truth, for whole families, whole communities, whole societies and fragments thereof. Storyteller is a role that includes intimacy with* Storytelling, *but is not the same thing. The tales of Storyteller carry the boney structure for new life to gather on, to gather around, to grow over in a distinct, culturally particular pattern. The tales of Storytelling are the everchanging answers to the questions, "what's happening, what's going on, right here, right now?" Storyteller teaches, trains, heals, with stories that change slowly and recreate, endure. Storytelling tumbles the heart's truths onto the dirt floor.*[8]

If you can imagine someone listening, hearing you out, then you can tell your stories on paper, or peck them into computers, or pluck them from the strings of your guitar. As the Storytelling constellation is struck and Storytelling erupts through you, you get to know the feeling. With practice you can recreate that magic on purpose, inventing the listening as well as the telling, and setting traps that will recreate your imaginings in the lives of others.[9]

Sometimes it is difficult to imagine even a single listener. Sometimes it is painful to remember having been received, heard, accepted, for the contrast that it makes to the usual responses we gather from the world and her people. When we invite Storytelling to come through, sometimes we can't hear anything at first. Then a stutter, cough, choke, like rusty old pipes that have long lain unused. The first trickles of wet sound may carry such brilliant red rust, we are fooled into thinking we are seeing wounding rather than healing. We stop action, pushing away birth, mistakenly believing we are pushing away death.

The juiciness, shagginess and ranginess of Storytelling remind us that birth and death are integral to the lives of each one of us, repeatedly buried and ever in need of fresh air. When we invite Storytelling to come through, and we hear silence, coughing, sputtering, see something wet and red, it is necessary for us to keep listening. The unpredictability of Storytelling is sure to come through, to honour us.

T*REE

I am a tree or even a whole great forest, it depends on my mood. Your voice is a wind that has come to stir and move me. When your images and your stories evoke mine, then I find myself in you, and all may become very clear or very confused. All our old quarrels may come to the surface. Then I must remind myself, you are not me in this instance. You are the wind and I am the tree/s. I must simply relax and allow you to pass through. Ruffling my hair. Touching me. I am not in control of you. But I am tall, I am wide. I am substantial. You are the wind. I can breathe.

The story you are telling is your story, even when the story I am hearing is my story. This is no accident. Stories come when it is time to be heard. I am not a leaf that can detach from my own life and escape along with you, riding your story to a new world. I can always pretend to be that leaf, I can pretend to be you. I can always listen and be transported. Yet I will always come back to my fullness, rooted in this one place, changed, informed, transformed, still tree/me.

When the wind of your voice begins to pull my hair out

by the roots, yank my guts a long way away, I can feel my limbs bunching up ready to pulverize you and demolish the wind. Here my choices lay. I can remove myself from you and the group and feel my feelings, listen to the stories of my limbs in privacy. I can rise up in challenge, turn your story into an heroic tale for two voices, intertwine the winds of our stories in public, and do battle. I can remember my limitlessness, and stretch myself to encompass the winds and the trees, the presence of my limbs and the pressures of your words, expand myself until you and I and the power of our stories all fit together in the same potent moment. I can remember my limits and allow the wind to push my tensions, secrets, agonies, lies and truths right out of me, streams of tears running down listening faces, trembling bodies bearing up wide open listening eyes, clearing passages, making stories' way clear again.

FOUR

The places where I am hurt most mark the places I am least tolerant, most vicious. Where I have been gravely injured and am most healed, these form my scant geography of wisdom. Where I have never been hurt at all, where I have never lacked for resource or nurture, these are the stories I find most difficult to perceive.

Storytelling leans against grey stucco, bits of broken glass embedded in a wall of concrete. The other woman heaves the window open, and something surges through, flies off.

Storytelling stands straight, something unwinding inside and pushing her upright. The other one clambers out the window and down, onto the street.

The moon and the stars, they are particularly strong, giving the streetlights a run for their money.

NOTES

1 Wendy Waring, correspondence.

2 Annharte, *Coyote Columbus Cafe* (Winnipeg: Moonprint Press, 1994).

3 Marketspeak sample, taken from Women's Press catalogue description of *By, For & About* anthology (1994).

4 Lisa Valencia-Svensson, "Mixed Race Women's Group—Dialogue One," *Miscegenation Blues: Voices of Mixed Race Women,* edited by Carol Camper (Toronto: Sister Vision Press, 1994).

5 Based on a true story, loosely.

6 *Concise Oxford.*

7 Ibid.; also reads as a brief author biography.

8 A large number of Aboriginal people in Canada today are disconnected from particular traditional cultural ways, as one intended and predictable result of policies of assimilation and institutionalized racism throughout this country's history. Oral traditions and the role of Storyteller do exist and carry forward in some modern First Nations (and some non-Aboriginal) communities. I am myself speaking/ writing from a marginal, heterodox, urbanized, fragmented-community point of view.

9 For example, written, published, performed works.

Harper's Moon

"Moon, moon," he says, taking my hand. "Come look."

I allow myself to be led through the basement apartment. At the back door we stop. As I look up into the sky, he drops my hand and lifts both of his own in a gesture of helplessness. "All gone!"

Just when I think it's a trick, he takes my hand again and gives me an encouraging shove. "Get it." We leave the house and walk around to the road. I look along the horizon, "Can't see . . ."

"There it is!" he cries, and grabs my legs with both hands. I pick him up, and we both gaze up at the moon in the pale evening sky.

"Broken," I say, referring to an observation he'd made about the moon, the evening before.

"Broken moon," he says.

"Look at that," I conclude, the adult, standing and gazing. "Broken moon."

Wild Girls: A Resurrection

In the beginning, first, from time out of mind, was the prairie. With her, the Aboriginal inhabitants built up cultures, traditions, histories, realities, more or less in harmony with, springing out of and interwoven with, the creatures, the plants, the lands and the weather that was home.

Then came the early trickles of immigrants out of Europe and elsewhere in the world, dependent upon, becoming neighbours with, exploiting and ultimately warring with, driving before them into smaller and smaller corners of the landscape, corners that had never existed before, all of the people, plants and animals which originally were expressions of, and inhabitants of, this place.

And then . . .

It was a hard year. I'd dropped two of my four classes at Arthur Meighan High School, and tended to skip out of the two I remained enrolled in, more days than not. Puberty, yes, and the shift from junior to senior high, but more than that. Some element of traumatic stress, a creeping kind of despair that things would ever/never change.

The days I skipped out were no more stimulating than

those I attended. I'd walk or hitch a ride into town and go to my friend Connie's place. Connie was a couple of years older than me, a drop-out, already married. She and Mike had had a very sad and romantic deathbed wedding, for her father, a sort of going-away present for him.

I'd sit around in the kitchen while Connie slept, Mike off working at the gas station. She'd get up, we'd drink instant coffee, watch soap operas. I smoked their cigarettes. I played with their kitten. Once in awhile Mike came home and we smoked pot in the early afternoon. Once Connie was mad at Mike, for something she wouldn't reveal, and brought out his beer. She and I sat on the floor playing caps all morning.

At some point the school counsellor was set on me, and I had to visit her a few times in her small office. A diminutive woman with black hair and blue eyes, she seemed to shift often in her feeling toward me: soft, maternal, beckoning; hard-nosed, calloused, hating; encouraging and friendly; angry and disdaining. My first visit to her office remains vividly impressed on me, the primary feelings of terror and suffocation, the fundamental fact that she had lured me into the room, and then closed the door behind me.

The first half of that visit must have been quite different for each of us. I do not know what she said, what she asked, how she made her approach. All I knew was that the door was closed, and in my panic, all I could do was look from her to the door, her, the closed door, over and over. I suppose in looking at her I must have gathered enough information to tell me I wasn't about to be beaten or raped. Eventually my focus widened enough to realize that there was a window behind me, with a view onto a snowy court-yard and other rooms of the school. By shifting in my chair and looking out the window, I was able to calm down enough to begin to hear what this adult was saying, and slowly come round to making coherent responses. She spoke a little bit about higher learning, jobs. She invited me to look through the calendars and the occupations file in her outer office.

The vice-principal called me in, too, a familiar face who'd moved up from teaching sciences at the junior high I'd attended. He was friendly, but clear. If I wanted to pass, I had to attend my classes. If I wanted to remain at school, I would have to stay on the school premises during school hours. Because I'd dropped half my course load already, he asked me to spend my free hours in the school library.

The previous semester I'd had good enough grades, especially in English. My teacher was an innovator, taught us a bit of Swahili, encouraged us to approach creatively even the most mundane assignments. She was new in town, still had a bit of the stink of the big city and a wider world clinging to her clothes. The librarian, who I began to see on a daily basis, was much quieter, more the muted sort of prairie person I was used to.

After weeks of random readings that left me dissatis-fied, I began to systematically pursue knowledge in a partic-ular area. The subject of my investigation, witchcraft. My earliest girlhood had been dedicated to the pursuit of good-ness through Roman Catholicism, and the several worlds that met in public schools and at Halloween intrigued me. All the literature available on witchcraft was Christian-based, some serious and some sensationalist, and much of it focussed wholly upon the Inquisition.

Bizarre accusations, weird confessions, investigations based on torment and mutilation, punishments that ended irrevocably in death. The things these girls and women did with Satan, for Satan, as Satan; the things the men of the Churches thought and said and did in pursuit of Satan, in their war against Satan, caused me to sit up in my chair dumbstruck, and to sink down into my seat in silent misery. One book, and one book only, took a scholastic and level approach, and in the thick of that scholar's language, I began to scent the lie. Is life really this weird? The answer this one out of perhaps a dozen authors writing across a span of centuries in both Europe and North America, the answer he seemed to be leading me to was, no, life in itself is not so weird, but be wary of the illusions of adults with power.

There was a big scene at my junior high school. At the time, I was convinced it shouldn't have involved me at all.

I was inexplicably called out of my class and told to go to the principal's office. I walked down the quiet hall, walked around the bear pit with its green carpeted seating, and stood inside the office door at the front counter. I was told to come in and wait. I saw my sister from the high school there, and gratefully moved to stand beside her. The school principal was there, and a couple of policemen. My father was there, too, not a good sign. Someone, the school counsellor perhaps, came and asked my elder sister to go and get our younger sister. The girl was in the staff lounge, hiding under the chairs and tables.

Later my sisters and I stood waiting outside the big glass doors at the front of the school. Our father remained inside a few more minutes. All the other children we knew carried on with their schoolwork. We went riding home in the middle of the day in our father's car: one furious adult male, three terrified teenaged girl children.

I remember riding home on the school bus, too, fending off the queries of the other kids: How come you weren't on the bus, how come you were called to the office, where is your sister? That must have come later, the next day. The afternoon remains a dull space, quick images of fury and tearing clothing, yells and pleading.

The evening itself I remember clearly, and sadly, with suppertime passing and my little sister still disappeared. A long slow disaster, my older sister's efforts at intercession ignored, my younger brothers quietly making a bag lunch and trying to slip it to the girl in the cellar, only to be foiled. Finally her naked body, white with shock and almost uninhabited, pulled from the cellar by our sister and our father.

Many years later these, or other allegations of a similar nature, were investigated by Interpol.[1] The investigator's hands were tied by the RCMP, investigating themselves in a small town, and by the doctor, the social worker, the school principal, the hospital staff, all of whom failed to keep accurate records of their interactions with my family, and, in the end, by the simple ordinariness of my dad. "If something like that had happened," the school principal is supposed to have said, "I certainly would have remembered it."

I know from the child's point of view that this is precisely the sort of thing a person forgets, automatically or with an effort, in order to survive. Things happen and we wrestle the information into unconsciousness. Or we go one better, and instead of first absorbing and then forgetting, as soon as we realize that danger's at hand we throw open both the front door and the cellar, shunting the information directly into that other place, storing it safely away from our usual day to day.

According to Alice Miller,[2] the adults—father, policemen, school principal and counsellor in this case, a doctor, social worker and hospital staff in another—collude because they were once harmed in just the same way. Acting out of the information they have gathered, stored, occluded, they participate unself-consciously, or only a little self-consciously, in horrendous acts/events of oppression. According to Rikki Sherover-Marcuse,[3] without that fundamental conditioning throughout childhood, the separations into *us* and *them,* targets and not-targetted groups, the systematic quashing of resistance to cruelties against ourselves and against others, not one of those people would have co-operated in the painful betrayal of our entire family, abandoning an adult lashing out and his child victims.

I am so impressed by my younger sister, her courage in resistance, in going to the principal's office to tell him a bit of the goings-on at our house. Whether she was fully expecting his belief, support and assistance, or was forced by circumstances to the point where she had to try one more time to get help for us, however hopelessly, she was obviously still able to think about what was happening, to discuss it with a friend, and to follow that friend's advice to tell an adult. How I survived was *book book book,* fantasy and escape, the country mouse nibbling on Thackeray. "This one's always got her nose in a book." *Don't even think about it.* But my younger sister did. She thought, she spoke out, she took action.

We were a mixed-race family, not quite Indians/not quite white, in the heart of the short-lived Republic of Manitobah, one of the seats of Métis revolution a century before. The authorities we dealt with were white. They were also all men against three young women, further colluding in the righteous suppression of wild girls.

Repression, suppression, oppression, leading to depression alternating with rage, and distrustful behaviour, and poor grades, to drug and alcohol abuse, and suicide attempts, all of which were then and are now used to complete the circle of silence, used to assasinate victims' characters, proof of our untrustworthiness, indications of our unworthiness altogether.

Depending on your era, you might say we were savages, paranoid, clutched in the throes of false memory/mass hysteria, even possessed by Satan . . . to accuse such an ordinary guy of making use of violence, sexual assaults, his male friends and root cellars, in the difficult task of child rearing. To accuse such an ordinary town of alternately ignoring and actively supporting such goings on.

The first summer our mother came to visit, I was digging my toes in the hot sand in our yard, terribly excited. My sisters and I had a plan. We appointed my older sister to approach our mother, to tell her how awful our father really was. She'd left him herself, it seemed a pretty sure bet she would listen.

My sister's look of defeat as she and our mother came walking down the lane was easy to perceive, her whole body yelling her failure.

"I started to tell her, but she just started shouting, *He promised he wouldn't do that any more! He promised!*"

The woman had shouted the teenager down. The issue was changed yet remained unaddressed. My mother's sense that her ex-husband was no good was confirmed once again. The subject of our safety didn't seem to come up anymore.

I was upset. I left the library or the classroom or wherever in the high school I'd been when the feeling came over me. I went into the girl's washroom. Shortly after, there was a knock on the door. I slipped into a stall and hid, feeling guilty and scared on top of whatever upset had driven me in there. The door to the washroom opened, and the voice of the blue-eyed school counsellor rang out, "Is there anybody in here?" The school principal's voice followed a moment later, "Is anyone here?"

I have the right to remain silent . . .

To my great horror, they came in and began a stall by stall inspection, discussing the physical condition of each and every ceramic bowl, metallic wall, swinging door. I sat silently on the back of a toilet, warring with myself, trying to decide to declare myself, to move, speak out, step out, and at the same time praying that somehow or other, they must stop, leave the room, miss me.

They did not. Their looks of incredulity, at finding me crouched in that stall, helped convince me: *I am unreal.*

The image I carried of myself for years was very much that of our little house on the prairie. Just as I carry much of Canada's history forward in my blood and flesh and bones, that house embodied waves of Canadian history and settlement, before it went up in flames.

Originally it was a small log cabin on the prairie, similar to many others in that area and throughout Canada's regions, built by representatives of the early waves of European immigrants or their disowned relations—the forgotten people, the Half-breeds and Métis. At the time that I lived there, it had been renovated, with pressed-board nailed to the walls inside and out, a single-storey L-shaped creation with two additions onto the original square.

There was a small green pump in the kitchen for drawing water. In the bathroom was a sink and bathtub with drains that led nowhere, and no water access, and a lidded wooden box with a metal bucket and toilet seat inside, that periodically would fill and have to be dumped in the bush out back. We took garbage to the same place, and my father once in a while would burn it away.

There was a root cellar accessed by a trap door in the floor of my father's tiny bedroom. Sometimes his bed hid the opening, sometimes it was visible as a rectangular line cut in the white linoleum. At one time, perhaps, the people who lived in the cabin would store a winter's supply of nourishment in that root cellar, to be drawn upon as needed. Most of the time, in my time, the cellar was unused, closed, empty, the only things down there being spider webs, soil and darkness, and the occasional, recalcitrant, pubescent daughter. People would drop in to visit and be none the wiser: "Where's your sister?" Silence, heavy seriousness, interrupted by some casual lie by our father.

Such was my self: an awkward creation with a thin brittle overlay and clumsy additions, centred on a deep hidden well where bad news was automatically thrown, without examination, and without any obvious signs to alert the visitor. Such is Christianity, constantly in the process of renovation, disdainful of the authentic world, disseminating fragmentation. Such is Canada as a whole, defined by a small group of overpriveleged persons, who never have to carry their own waste out, who go on obliviously reigning and naming without reference to those who are pushed to the margins, shoved into corners, trapped inside root cellars.

Goodness will never win against evil. That split is an irresponsible division of reality.

My little town has a long history, part of a group of insular settlements co-existing on an arbitrary stretch of endless prairie. We lived outside the town, among an even mix of European and mixed-blood farmers. Between us and the town were an armed forces base, a small Indian reserve and the Trans-Canada highway. Then came the town itself where, since the closing of the local one-room schoolhouses, we were all bussed in for educational purposes. To the north and west were Hutterite colonies and Métis communities and more small towns and villages settled by a variety of peoples, and large and small Indian reservations scattered out in every direction. Finally, there was the world that seeped in from down east and down south, through the television set, at the drive-in, and via the hefty newspapers trucked in from Winnipeg. There were ways and places where these several distinct societies met, overlapped; there were as many or more differences and gaps that, for a girl already several times displaced, felt dangerous.

NOTES

1 Interpol, the international police, became involved when one of my siblings, then living overseas, brought charges against our father.

2 Alice Miller, a psychoanalytically trained German writer, reveals a fascinating process of "deprogramming" through the course of her many books. She is an outspoken critic of pedagogy and the systemic oppression of children, and the rampant denial of child abuse in European-based societies.

3 Rikki Sherover-Marcuse was an American anti-racist activist, who in the 1980s developed the Unlearning Racism theory and methods discussed further in the following essays.

The Country-Born

'BREED. HALF-BREED. MÉTIS. MESTIZA. COUNTRY-BORN

I am a person of mixed Native and European heritages.

Fundamentally what I have inherited is a good deal of information about the various European traditions from which I come, and racist denial of the existence of my Native ancestry. This is not unusual; in working with other people of mixed European/non-European heritages, I have found it common that the European is promoted at the expense of—and in a way that erases—the non-European. This is not exclusively true for all multi-ethnic families/people. Many are raised with a solid understanding of who they are and who/where they come from. Those who, like me, are raised in the white community *as whites,* who are not provided with true information about who we are, are caught up in shame-based family systems, a direct result of colonization, of racist conditioning taking place in a racist society.

Our situation is very similar to that of Native people taken from their homes and communities by various "welfare" bodies, and fostered, adopted or otherwise taken over by/into the white community as children, and deprived of information about and contact with their original group/ways/people. The difficulties for one whose *information* about oneself does not accurately describe or explain oneself, and the denial by family members that this information is inadequate or untrue, can be summed up in a few words: it is *crazy-making*.

THE PLIGHT OF THE NOT QUITE WHITE

The challenge: To grapple with the dissonance, to step beyond what has been agreed upon as "the truth," fragmented as it is, and to notice very carefully what my body says, how I am feeling. To surrender my defenses enough, to trust self and life enough that I am able to connect with my gut and think the unthinkable. To put a little space between my mother and myself, my father and myself, my siblings and myself, and within that space to bring out, look at and sort through what is true for me.

The entire point of denial is to make pivotal and fundamental truths "unthinkable." Denial is a survival technique, used to deal/not deal with threatening information. The hardest point initially is to have the thought, to observe or entertain the possibility of a different reality. Saying that thought out loud can also feel very hard, fraught with danger, like stepping off a cliff.

The impact of dissonance, of embodying opposed information, and the emotional impact with which that information was initially shared—laid in, embedded, imposed—is to frequently feel inauthentic, like a liar. Am I making it up? Given the way I was raised, frequently told I was lying even when, to my knowledge, I wasn't, the question is potent. This is my guide: No matter how difficult the transition is from one belief to another, I can tell flights of fancy from reconstructed reality by how I feel about myself and my world. Hard as it is to acknowledge violence, or sexual abuse, by acknowledging those things and their impact on me, I feel more right in the world, more at ease. I understand now the results, how I am.

No issue has been more powerful than reclaiming my Native ancestry. It is fundamental and provides a context for understanding everything else. It is also something I need to know on a daily basis, as an urban dweller. I am frequently asked about my ethnic background, skin colour, race. I am more visible than my forebears intended me to be. I like to believe I am everything they secretly hoped I would be.

Passing

The decision to "pass" as exclusively European descended is not a simple matter of delusion, of "wannabe." It is one of very few options for survival of mixed-race people in a virulently racist society.

Those of us descended from people who chose, even within their own famillies, to pass, need to remember this. The anger I have felt at having a perfectly normal, and to me acceptable, ancestry skewed and distorted into a painful blob of hurt, doubt and denial, the rootless and directionless rage I have inherited—these are my issues, my problems, my responsibilities. The ability to imagine the pressures brought to bear on my ancestors, only generations away, to the point where they denied themselves and erased themselves, is necessary. Whatever was done was done for the purposes of survival; it was the best option available to the individual at that time.

Racist denial is not restricted to individual people and families. Canada as a whole continues in a state of barely challenged denial of the existence of Native peoples, and—where it is admitted that we do exist—of the exploitation and derogation of Native peoples now and for many centuries past. The history of First Nations people in Canada, and the aggressive policies of cultural and economic genocide the Canadian and provincial governments and society have long employed against Native people, is far from common knowledge. The language of media reports on current events consistently *others* "the Natives" from the audience addressed, and this use of language, layered upon the massive ignorance of specific historical repression, aggravates the dissociation and exclusion of First Nations people from the "multicultural" society. The frustration accumulated through centuries of thwarted attempts to make change through legal, "legitimate" channels, is split off from the memory/knowledge of the historical struggle, and thus perceived as a rootless and bizarre attribute of First Nations people: *hostile Indians, the natives are restless.* Racism and racist denial are a part of the fabric of Canadian society. Denial on the societal level is, as it is on the individual and familial levels, similarly *crazy-making.*

OPPRESSION

Internalized racism and, more generally, internalized oppression, is a fundamental concept here.[1] The idea is that racism (any oppression) is a mixture of fear, ignorance and misinformation, held in place by a glue of unfelt (and unexpressed) feelings and undigested (unevaluated) information.

It works like this. A child is playing in the grass. Three other children come by and begin verbally to bait and belittle the single child, calling her "ugly," "stupid," "little Indian" and so on. Children automatically recognize mistreatment in patently abusive situations. We recognize, until we are trained not to, when abuse is happening.

The child responds at first with amazement. "No, I'm not. I'm not ugly. I'm not stupid." She is, however, little, and Indian, so she's caught: there's a grain of truth to their accusations and this can be painfully confusing. She becomes frustrated, angry; she leaps up and yells back, "*You're* stupid. *You're* ugly." The odds are three to one, but her self is at stake. The situation escalates. The children become more intensely abusive, she continues to fight back, until someone —the girl alone, or one of the others—is moved to fight physically. It ends where it ends, a typical childhood confrontation.

We might not like to call this attack by children a racist attack, but it is. Obviously the children who initiated the attack have already been taught the fundamentals of oppressive behaviour. They are testing out and practising the roles they will need to get by in this society and this (dominant) culture. The child alone is also being taught: she is being asked to play out the victim role. If she doesn't get the support she needs to understand what has happened to her, she will very likely pull her brother's hair or call her sister ugly in the very near future, in an attempt to relieve the tension left by the experience, and to practise the only other role that is obvious and available.

Oppression is a prejudice that is socially sanctioned, backed by the force of convention, society, the law (in theory and/or as practised).[2] If the group of children in our story are Euro-descended, and the child alone is Native-descended (in whole or in part), then society *sanctions* the abuse. The incident becomes just one thread in a seamless web of similar abuses. It is racism. If, as is possible, the initiators of the attack are also Native, this is called "internalized racism": the children have internalized—learned—society's images of Indians and the racist right conduct/right attitude toward Indians. They are playing their knowledge out against and upon one another. Internalized racism operates completely at the expense of the individuals involved and at the expense of all Native people and communities.

TAKING EXPERIENCE IN

However the fight in the grass ends, it ends eventually. The girl will go home, or to some place safe, and try to find a way to deal with the hurt she has received, to get some information that will make the confrontation make sense— make it digestible.

Children are in almost every way identical to adults;

their development and size, life experience and (in particular) social power are the few distinctions. Of course, the little girl will think about the event, and feel about it, either until someone can assist her in making sense of it or until she gives up hope of finding that assistance and must repress (deny) the event, in whole or in part, and get on with her life.

How we make sense of our experiences is crucial to our being in the world. If we can find someone, as children or as adults, to listen to us and stay by us while we digest our life experiences, we will be more healthy and more free in all ways. The process is completely natural and spontaneous. When we have an experience, and when all goes well, we digest it and are nourished by it.

This digestion is a wholistic process, and involves whatever body-expressions needed to take in the experience fully and return to a balanced state. The expressions that are more or less visible include shaking, crying, sobbing, raging, hitting and kicking, sweating, talking, giggling, laughing, even yawning.[3] Digestion also includes thinking, intuition and insight, turning the experience into useable information about people and the world, information that can be used to guide future conduct and understanding. This can include observations of interpersonal dynamics, observations about feelings, thoughts and sensations, and new words or concepts learned from the interaction. It is as much a physical as a mental or emotional process, and as much social as personal: with the caring attention of another person, the whole process moves more rapidly and thoroughly.

To the degree to which useful support is unavailable to us, we become burdened, beaten, and progressively shut-down. We carry the harmful experiences with us, collecting layer upon layer of undigested experiences and faulty conclusions about ourselves and our worlds. They overtake our lives, to the point where abuse becomes the reference point, and positive experiences slide off our backs like water, leaving little or no impression.

If our child alone is lucky, her family will have retained or developed some healing ways of being there for each other. If not, she will go home to elders who are carrying the same sort of pain and confusion and rage that she is, accumulated over all of their added years, amplified by the creeping despair of not finding a way to change things. They will be unable to help her. They are just trying to survive. That is the best that can be done for now.

My Family

At this point, I am convinced that my father doesn't "know" that he is Native.[4] I think perhaps one of his brothers, the most visibly Native of the bunch, "knows," but he has never spoken to me about it. My father's sister has been knowing/not knowing it for years, she has told and denied so many times I get dizzy thinking about it. All of this tells me that their parents denied the truth to them, which is exactly the crazy-making formula that caused so much confusion and pain in my own life. The violence, the sexual abuse and every other oppressive and "crazy" thing that happened to and around me is intimately connected to that crazy-making denial and the crazy-making racist oppression that parented it.

The poverty of my family and our various expressions of internalized racism, including self-erasure, are shared by many other Native families. For Native people raised in Native communities, there is the further oppression of their communities as a group, the shared poverty and shared results of racism and internalized racism.

The hope behind and the key benefit to successfully "passing" is escaping oppression, by distancing from targetted groups and by refusing to acknowledge one's connection to people who are targetted, to their issues and realities. This chosen alienation is acutely experienced by the offspring who are "throwbacks": who are not received by the world in the way they have been taught to expect, who lack the information to help them make sense of their lives. The danger for all of us is the powerlessness we experience as a group, because those who ultimately benefit socially and economically from this successful "divide and conquer" continue unchallenged.

Next Generation

For my own sanity and for the welfare of my children, it has been crucial, pivotal and inescapable: I must reclaim my Native heritage, my roots, my Indian-ness. I look at myself and my family, and pick through the little bits I've been told about my father's people. I seek out information about the history of Canada and Native North Americans, especially that told from a Native perspective. I sift through all of this and try to hear the words beyond the silence, to see the Indian in me, to be aware of the traditional and tribal roots under the avalanche of Euro-domination. Like my uncle, I am one of the more "visible" of my generation. It is essential for me to talk about it, first in the safety of workshops and support groups, then to my friends, those in my family I'm closest to, then strangers, acquaintances. I go back over my life and find countless incidents where I have received help, and/or abuse, from people who recognized me at a time when I did not recognize myself. I am able to think about the times I took part in the racist erasure and internalized oppression of other Native people, and to feel and express the pain of that, and to begin to understand how to be there for my people and for myself.

'BREEDS

I am one hundred percent who I am. I am a blending of these parts: I am an Anishnabe woman, I am Sioux. I am a Scottish woman, a French-Belgian woman. I'm Irish. There is no such thing as "just Canadian," unless it is, as Duke Redbird claims, people like me, us, Métis, Half-breeds.[5]

Many people don't know who they are, don't know their own histories or the tribal roots from which they come. It is important for us to look into the realities that formed our forebears: the residential schools, anti-potlatch and similar laws in Canada; the Highland Clearances in Scotland and the attempted decimation of Welsh, Irish and many other cultures; the colonizations and forced trade; the "world" wars; the inquisitions. As we inform ourselves of our histories and the histories of our families and peoples, we gain not only understanding in an abstract way, but in a gut way that is very immediate and empowering. Just as physical cues persist and resurface through generations, other traditions are being carried on, without the worldviews and community-basis that created them.

When we know who we are and where we come from, we gain the power to know who we are not, to make decisions about the quality of our lives, to make demands and implement strategies for changes therein.

"Generic Exotic"

As a friend said, I look like a "generic exotic."[6] Those of us who fall into this category receive a variety of responses in the world, limited only by other people's imaginations.

We are often treated as suspect and frequently questioned about our heritages. We receive both help and abuse based on who we are perceived to be, whether or not the perception bears any relation to who we really are.

We exist in Native and in white communities, raised under an endless variety of conditions and traditions. Many of us have also participated in a tradition which is uniquely our own: to be accepted by no one, claimed by neither side, spurned by both.

The centuries of abuse perpetrated on Native people, communities and nations by Euro-descended people, communities and nations has, not astonishingly, generated a good deal of pain and hostility that has yet to begin to heal. Who am I, then, if I am both?

Within the Western mindset, we are always asked to choose, to be one or another of an endless array of polar opposites. People with multiple heritages bow to the pressure to choose at the risk of great damage to our beings. We are both Native and European, we take part in some of the experiences of both groups.

We only appear to be *generic exotics*. Each of us is particular. We are not nearly as exotic as our full-blood European relatives. For each and every one of us, this place is our home place, our history encompasses the histories of all Native North American Nations and all the invading and immigrating Nations. We do belong here.

CONTINENTAL DRIFT

The theory of tectonic plates, of continental drift in geology, seeks to explain the movement of continents: the birthing of islands and the throes of mountain-building pressures in the land, volcanic activity where hot rock from below surges forth into the world with a roar, lands pushing together and shuddering, the tension in their coming together shaking the creatures who live on their surface and sometimes killing them. It is a lot about strife, but it is also about the creation of place, the constant movement and change that is life on this earth. Beautiful, new and unique entities are born at every moment. We take part in this.

The history of Native/Europeans in the Americas — Métis, Mestizo, Half-breeds, the Country-Born — is intimately connected to that of Native/Asians, African-Americans, and all other multi-ethnic people. We are also intrinsically connected to all of our full-blood relatives, all over the world.

By using our imaginations and seeking to conduct our lives in such a way that we foster the world spirit rather than rupture or deny it, we can make the radical changes required. All beings rely upon our respectful attention.

NOTES

1 Unlearning Racism theory. Unlearning Racism is a particular approach to anti-racist work, developed in the 1980s by the late Rikki Sherover-Marcuse of California. This approach combines work on the individual and group levels, emotional as well as theoretical, and is usually presented in a workshop format. Re-evaluation Co-counselling is a form of peer-counselling developed by Harvey Jackins and others. Unlearning Racism shares much of the basic theory of Re-evaluation Co-counselling, but has evolved as a distinct entity focussed on eliminating racism.

2 Unlearning Racism theory.

3 Re-evaluation Co-counselling theory.

4 My sister puts forward some convincing arguments that my father's generation is fully aware of our ancestry.

5 Duke Redbird, *We Are Metis* (Ontario Metis & Non Status Indian Association, 1980).

6 Sybila Valdevieso, thanks.

Wasting Time

I feel like a dog on a chain.

I feel like a caged dog.

I was rubbing my sister's neck, her shoulders, as she lay on the floor before me. The baby was jealous and kept crawling onto my lap, sitting on her head or in the small space between her head and my legs, standing on her braid, pulling at my layers of clothes in search of a nipple.

My sister kept making jokes at the dinner party the night before, and I kept thinking about them now. About nursing on our mother, who is fifty-four years old. This sister, she is older than me. She is jealous of my babies, threatens to steal them from me, also a joke.

Our oldest sister had a baby six weeks ago, and I had the dinner party last night to say hello to the baby and the dad, and hello again, good-bye, to our sister. Even though we spent a number of hours together we hardly said boo to each other; too many babies, an ocean of children's demands flowing between us.

You know how women are after their first. It's like our lives cave in and the reality of our oppression, as women, as parents, and in particular as very young children, all of it rushes to the surface and at the same time, slams down on us, hits home. And somehow, within these very same moments, we are suffused with a sense of greatness, this sense of goodness/gracious, of touching Source and being touched by Source. Embodying the power of full self and Beyond Self, yet so very fragile: we are left with a pile-up of experience that we really don't have the words to describe. The first couple of years see the ideal and the real coming into collision in a really big way, again and again, all across our bodyminds.

I remember the feeling of being near but not with. I could clearly see the place she had gone to. I thought if we'd just had a minute I could tell her I knew what it was like, but that minute never came.

So the next day my other sister comes back and she asks me to rub her neck and I do. I enjoy it at first, but then her similarities to my father begin to strike me. I begin to have visual flashes, him and her, her and him. For long moments I don't know whose neck and shoulders I'm rubbing, don't remember if I volunteered to do this or if this is further duress. The baby's jealousy and demands add to my distress.

The baby's jealousy. The baby's demands. My distress.

To whom do I owe this nurture? I tried for many years to be my mom's best friend and have only recently given that up. I think about and try not to think about the fullness of my relationship with this woman before me, this sister, try to slide my glance away from past violations, intimidations, tricking me with words, putting her mouth on my breast, burning me on both arms with cigarettes. I try to force bygones to be bygones but they push up into present time again and again.

I like a little mothering myself, when I can get it. But mostly it is the mothers mothering others and the baby-identified grown-ups—like my sister, my father, my mother —standing around at the centre of the world, competing with the new lives coming up. In the end it has nothing to do with children, and a lot to do with *who gets taken care of*, with domination and subservience, with power.

Somehow I've become the kind of person other people tell their dreams to, and their nightmares. Each day I'm dragged, usually willingly, through the deepest recesses of other people's psyches. Look at this, look what we have here, what do you make of it? It all relates back to sexual abuse, physical torture, terror or simple hatred. What do you make of that? The tyranny of the bigger one in this world.

I got a note, no really just a copy of a flyer, from an ex-lover who is having an art show. It's called "Human Lights." The timing is interesting. It was he who painted my gaunt dog, the one I wrote about so often in those days. I rarely write about it now, I rarely feel it, but today it's come up like a storm, it's arrived with a snarl. The dog is caged, I am dog, out of the quiet I rise up, viciously angry.

Once upon a time I dreamed the dog, often. Then I began to write the dog, its portraits. The last dog image that came through my dreams was striking: I am walking through a typical muddy yard, rural you know, but like a farm yard where lots of vehicles come and go. A big space. I see the dog chain, really long, lots of it, all laid out in a neat line, across the mucky surface, disappearing into a wide muddy puddle and continuing out the other side and away. I am curious about it being under the water, concerned about rust or who knows? Anyway, I grab hold of the chain and pull. As it comes away from the water, I notice things dangling from it. As I pull some more, I see it is several packages of store-bought meat, neatly cut and clearly wrapped and attached to this very long chain and dropped into the puddle. The feeling of horror is indescribable. Tidy meat on a chain. I drop the chain with a splash, shaken to the core.

Revulsion.

An interesting feeling.

I finally told my sister I couldn't do this any more. I said I wasn't feeling very well which, by then, of course, was true. After she left, I sat quietly, sipping coffee, nursing the baby, smoking a cigarette.

A friend called and we started talking babies. Her boss was very upset for most of the time that his wife was pregnant. A co-worker sniped, "He's worried his Black blood will show up." I mentioned my sister and the dislocation of first-time fathers, first-time mothers, and my friend told me about someone else whose sister finally told her, "Ma wished you'd never been born, she wished she'd had an abortion."

"All my life I knew that was true," her friend said, rocking the infant close and sitting in a mist of great sorrow. My own youngest sister had been hurt so many times, she tried to find relief/reprieve by killing herself. Our mother, driving her to the hospital, said, "Look, I've been through this enough times with your sister. If you're going to do it, just do it."

In a fit of compassion.

As I say to my own son, clutching my coffee cup and

peering through the ever-present haze of cigarette smoke, as I say to my young companion when I'm feeling angry and pressed, as I rarely say to the adults around me, with a glare: "Don't waste my time."

Speak Out, For Example

One day I dropped by unexpected at a friend's place, knock knock. As she opened the door, she said with pretend irritation, "What do you want *now*?" When she saw it was me, she laughed. "Sorry. I thought it was my mutt . . ."

No, dear woman, it is not your mutt. It is someone else's mutt at the front door.

At the time I was too surprised, too unsafe, to do more than focus my attention carefully on whatever had brought me to her door in the first place. But the incident has stayed with me, the sort of sting that crystallizes much into its simplicity.

In 1988, I attended an Unlearning Racism workshop presented by Rikki Sherover-Marcuse. Since then, I have attended and led many such workshops. I have met a diversity of women and men with mixed/multiple heritages. I will take a few minutes now to talk about racism, specifically from a mixed or multiple heritage person's point of view, but there is no way I can speak for everyone. The format I will use is that of a Speak Out exercise, as taught by Rikki Sherover-Marcuse—a tool for educating people, a platform for people targetted for oppression to speak *and be heard*. I will address three points:

1 What I want you to know about me and my people.
2 What I never want to hear again.
3 What I expect of you as my allies.

Your job is just to listen. If you are also a mixed-race person, take some time to answer the questions for yourself. Remember to leave space for your feelings, because feelings and experience are essential and need to be channelled, embraced, cherished. If you are not a mixed-race person, please repeat back whatever you remember of what I said in response to points one and three, and bear point two in mind—but remember, I really don't want to hear it again.

WHAT I WANT YOU TO KNOW
ABOUT ME AND MY PEOPLE

About me.   I am a person of mixed Native and European ancestry. I know lots about my European ancestry and almost nothing about my Native heritage: this is one impact of racism. I was raised in a white community as a white working-class person. As children, when I or my sisters or brothers attempted to talk about our relationship to or similarities with Native people, we were punished. Our parents seemed to believe in lies about our ancestry and we were forced to believe, or to pretend to believe, the same; this is one aspect of internalized racism. At the same time that this white-out policy was in effect, we were constantly being recognized by friends and by strangers, by people not under the sway of the family's survivalist lies. This combination of messages meant that I needed to sort a world of responses to a Métis person through my insecure identity of whiteness. Confusion, dissonance, incongruity, self-doubt, endless inadequacy, deep shame were the results. The process of healing has been a tearing down and tearing up of almost every constituent belief I held about myself and my world, and a re-centring in the truth of bodymind, of spirit, a re-awakening of my deep self and a reconstruction of my social self, my being in the world, on this new/old/original foundation.

About my people.   People with multiple ethnic heritages are an extremely diverse bunch. Our looks are diverse, our habits and heritages diverse, our knowledge of ourselves, our ancestries, our traditions, our families are diverse. To use the example of mixed Native and non-Native heritage people, some of us are raised on reserve, in the bush, in small towns, on farms, in cities, and/or any combination of these places; as Indians, as Métis, as 'breeds, as whites, Blacks, Asians; with great pride, with great shame, with full knowledge, in complete ignorance, with double and triple messages about who we are and about our place in the world. For many of us, the greatest source of racism, hurt and shame is our own families. For many of us, our families are the cradles of safety against racist abuse and rejection from the outside world.

Big issues.   Passing, and the not-Black-enough, not-Indian-enough hassles we put on ourselves, collect from other people. "Where are you from?" "Are you two related?" In terms of multigenerational denial and complicities, it is important for us to acknowledge the privileges of European people, the very real dangers to our physical survival as Indians, Blacks, Asians in the context of the Americas. The decisions of family members to deny who we are do not come easy, they are meant to save lives. It is one strategy.

Further layers of complexity get laid in when we are raised by people not targetted for oppression in the same way we are, like the Black child of the white woman who affectionately called him "mutt" to her Métis girlfriend. Our worlds differ fundamentally, in how we are received and who we are received by. There are basic truths and survival skills a person of colour must learn that white parents don't know about.

Possibly the most difficult issue for people of mixed heritage is that of belonging, and a part of that is safety: constantly testing the waters to see how I am seen, and what the perceiver's response to their perceptions might be. The wide world laid open for people with multiple heritages is a well of potential, centred in a sometimes perilous terrain. The sliding identity that can be so difficult at first can become a very powerful tool for peacemakers.

What I Never Want to Hear Again

Mutt. Half-breed. Heinz 57. Wannabe.
I never want to face another door opened by a mother who calls the child of her own body by racist names.

WHAT I EXPECT OF YOU AS MY ALLIES

What is an ally? An ally can be a friend, family member, co-worker, complete stranger, but none of these is automatically an ally. Ideally, an ally is someone who is aware of their own issues of hurt and oppression, accumulated over the years, and is healing, who is aware of the differences between themselves and another, who cherishes that other person, intervenes when they can to interrupt intimidations and attacks against them, supports them in their struggles against both oppression and internalized oppression. The possibility for every one of us to be allies against oppression is always present. Mistakes are made, and as allies we commit ourselves to confronting rather than ignoring them, and doing the emotional and other kinds of work needed to correct and clean up mistakes and misunderstandings.

Notice the great pain carried by many, many, many mixed heritage people. Notice our strength, our great pride. Notice us, everywhere in the world.

Don't make assumptions about the heritage of other people, thinking that if someone looks white, looks European, that they want to hear your racist jokes in a buddy-buddy fashion. Or conversely, if someone looks Indian, that they are an automatic font of deep wisdom via continuous ancient tradition.

As an ally you must never expect me to choose sides, because I am all sides. You must never silence the parts of me that need to be given voice, especially when the parts of me do not agree. I need the fullness of that space to sort out the contradictions of my life experience, to solidify a grounded and well-rounded sense of who I am, my place, and what my work in the world might be, based on that reality.

What I expect of my allies is not to divide up the world by race and caste without acknowledging that every single boundary is blurred, and that these blurrings occur not only out of a conquerer mentality, but also out of love and need, and that these blurrings have a name: we are called human beings. What I expect of my allies is to expect full pride from me, and to foster it.

We all learn the same racist crap and we all need to stop perpetrating it on ourselves, on one another and on the young people. Participating in the diminishing of ourselves and of others is how we have learned to survive. It takes conscious effort, storming and weeping, and courageous collaboration to turn things around. There are many things that each one of us can do, actions large and small can be taken, alone, together. Heal old wounds, demand the fullness of life. Listen carefully. Speak out, for example.

Dear Zorka

I'm missing you today.

This summer, I sat with an old best friend for a few minutes. Her name is Kathy and she is Métis. I remembered I liked her a lot, but her beauty took me by surprise. I sat there silent and embarrassed at first, as she stood by my table in the bar. She is stunning. Her posture, her hair and complexion, and above all her eyes—beauty. Perfection.

At first I only felt sadness. All I could remember was writing to her after I'd first moved away, and her writing me back, "You can write to me if you want. But I don't think we have anything in common." Perhaps that's when I first forgot she was beautiful.

Loneliness is like a pack of dogs in pursuit of me. I lose them for a while, or forget them. Soon enough I look up and notice their ragged forms standing at the edge of the light and at the edge of the darkness. Or I wake up to the sound of their running through the trees toward me. Now that I'm older, I know they fear me too, are only half fascinated. I'm relatively safe if I can hold out, refuse to bolt and run.

My sister had told me some of Kathy's troubles. As I looked at her and, after she sat beside me, listened to her

voice and laughter, sensed her beside me, enjoyed her asking after me and asked after her in turn, heard that she'd had
two sons like I do, but older . . . I was able to separate some
of her sadness from my sadness, to notice her determina-
tion toward joy, to separate her from some alien being who
had no troubles, was perfect and had nothing in common
with me.

I began to rise toward her as one who, for a while, had
been her best friend. I told her my good news.

"I have a book coming out."

"A what?"

We fumbled with conversation for a while, her acting
like she'd never heard the word "book" before. Only now
do I remember that she once got an *A* on an English assignment by handing in a story I'd written. It was called "Death
of an Old Man," a portrait of isolation, loss, missed connections. That was years ago, anyway, what are friends for?
Through our conversation I could see that, in some ways,
she had been right. What I have in my heart is not what she
has in her heart, even though we are both fine people and
used to be best friends.

I think of her when I think of you, sometimes.

Your people are in the news a lot these days, and I wonder about the city where I knew you, and all the ex-patriates
there. I wonder if any of your brothers or sisters have gone
back to ex-Yugoslavia, to have a hand in the homeland's
unsettling, resettling.

Perhaps that's why you come to mind, the headlines call
you back. But I don't think of you in terms of your ethnicity,
primarily. I think of you as a best friend, a long-standing one

who, with some very grand flourishes, broke my heart, blew my mind, played a deft hand in my dislocation.

I'm not writing to blame you, to drag it all up. I'm writing to you out of my love and my loneliness, out of all the sweet devotion that remains after all the cataclysms and the many years of silence. I am not writing to you because you broke my heart.

There are more places in me that were befriended by you than in any other friendship I've had with women or with men. Excepting the organic growth of my relationships with my children and my siblings, there is only you as an icon of knowing, as near a parallel to me outside myself as I've found in the universe.

Notice.

So when I'm lonely and tired of talking to myself, I turn to the image of you, a chimera, a ghost to lean on.

Writing to you is, I know, a foolish activity. You will have grown and changed—in fact, you did already and that's why I said good-bye to you the first time. My bet and gamble is, what I tell myself is, that you've grown and changed back into a woman I could love and talk to again. To someone who could read this and not write back that we have nothing in common, but pick up the threads of this and that, tell stories, draw out the echoes.

Just as Kathy embodies the prairies and the country and a society from which I came but never felt I belonged, you embody the lakes and the city and a society in which I almost learned to take part.

You are, like me, an outsider. You taught me the term DP,[1] which has proved to be a key. Kathy represents the self

I could have become, had my family salvaged pride.[2] You parallel the self I am, with a war-torn family and a being forged by implosion.

I would like to find you again.

I would like to set my heart and mind at rest, to pick up that history one more time and cradle those shipwrecked girls to my breast, as a big person this time, as a guide. The encouragement, the intelligence we shared, the common comfort: these are potent paths to healing. I would like to encircle us both with my arms and tell us so, tell us we are very good girls, and deserving. *You girls will exist beyond time, as your lives change inside you and around you. What you are doing is a good thing. What you are sharing will endure. Your strategies are among the very best for survivors.*

Disaster and girlhood. These are the two sides of the coin that drew us together, and also the price we paid on our parting. Disastrous girlhood, and we two struggling up armed only with our pride, our creativity, our minds and each other.

Of all the disappointments and mystifications unmasked, the loss of you to God is most bitter. How we could travel together so far, grasping one another's hands so tightly, climbing through one another's minds to verify the geography, only to lose one another at that final bend where you took a leap of faith, and I turned away from the edge and from you also, preferring the feeling of my feet on the solid Earth Mother.

It was the sexuality you hated. In this context, mine. When I told you I had had sex with a woman friend, you attacked me, publicly and viciously. When I turned away from you finally, I had a man on my arm, one who would cup my belly as he slept, who lay for hours with me in bed, singing.

I have since leapt into chasms myself, dangled through air and ocean and even slipped between layers of earth and gone swimming. Of all the goddesses, gods and demons I have dealt with, none of them was yours, and none of them had a word from you for me.

So where are you now?

And why does your ghost keep coming back to see me?

Perhaps you are dead, and it is time that I told your story. Perhaps you are alive, and telling your children about me. Perhaps I will find out, or your ghost will fade away for good this time, or you will suddenly arrive to tell me about our friendship from your point of view, and I will somehow be shamed. I don't know. I can't even tell if it is me who keeps resurrecting you, or you who haunts me, or if somehow our souls have combined and each time you come to mind it is a struggle and a labour, as in birth, attempting to separate. Two girls with one heart, half a continent and now a full ocean apart, stumbling through life with their wits about them and their bodies in order and their lives grown to adulthood, but with only half a heart, and their souls bound up with some stranger not seen for a decade.

The calamities that beset us before we found one another and struggled for breath, for life together—perhaps they'd destroyed more of us than we were able to admit. Perhaps the healing we did together, without guidance, mistakenly melded our spirits or hearts into one, and at our parting each of us tried to wrest it from the other, crying through our teeth, "It's mine!"

If so, then you and I may still have something in common.

The possibility that I was the victor, who made off with

the remains of your heart just when you'd decided to give it to someone or something else, has never occurred to me before. That in the wrenching apart, I may have taken away more than I lost, and it is for this that your ghost returns . . .

I worry about your corporeal self. What happened to the girl I said good-bye to?

These are just the sort of questions we two could grapple with, and settle satisfactorily. How am I to grapple with them alone? Anyway, I won't. I'm not so alone anymore. I have taken several goddesses to heart and it is through them, Her, Goddess, that I climb to understanding now.

My understanding is still piecemeal, in progress. But I am still alive and I count that as a victory, good guidance. I pose my questions and always get answers, even though the answer is, almost always, *relax, let go*. Even though, like the mother of a toddler, Her answer is often simply to distract me, to redirect my attention to something I'd never noticed before, or to something seen and discounted.

I am in China now, far away from you. Did I mention it?

I haven't dreamed about you lately. I did dream that I was learning Chinese, which is good because in the non-dreaming world I am shut out a lot by my ignorance. Thus the loneliness with which this letter began.

You sang to me, "everybody's got a hungry heart," introduced me to Costello. A working-class boy made good. Zorka, we are all good, it's an inborn quality. The poverty is something we live in or pass through, but it is not us. Although my heart hungers, I would never devour you, if I was at all aware of what I was doing.

If in the past you have felt you lost something to me, I

surrender it to you again, and with it unleash your spirit from entanglement with mine. I am my own person. You are your own person. Separate.

And still I love you and miss you, wonder where and who and how you are, and your brothers and sisters too. In the past I have offered you sanctuary, and you have been my sanctuary for many years. In releasing you, I cherish the hope that I will encounter you again.

Or, perhaps, simply leave myself open
for a
new
best
friend
to walk into my heart.

Kaoshiung Milk Bar,
Taipei
1992

NOTES

1   Displaced Persons.
2   I'm talking idealized images here, which may depart quite a bit from experienced realities.

At Salem

At the Salem Picnic I walk alone through a sea of cars parked at the back of the hall. I am looking for the kids my age, who must be here somewhere. The sun beats down on the bleached grass and powdery dirt yard, and the voices of people at play carry far.

I have been to baseball picnics before, though never at this particular hall. I am sure I'll find a few familiar faces, around the next corner perhaps. I am happy until some old iron grip traps my arm and I am halted. I turn to find an old man with steel grey hair sticking out from his head, his cold blue eyes staring into mine with complete malice.

"Come here."

"What for?"

"You'll see what for."

"No. I can't."

Menacing voice, tightening grip. "You're coming."

He walks away without loosening his hold, he is dragging me in his wake, we are moving in a direction quite different from the path I had chosen.

"Don't. *Don't.*"

Into the churning of fear and confusion overtaking my

small frame, a new voice drops three powerful words from behind us.

"Let her go."

This is my father's voice. I am deeply grateful. My father comes to stand beside me, putting his big hand on my shoulder.

The old man is a stranger to me but not, I think, to my father. The old man takes a few long moments before relinquishing his deadly grip on my narrow arm. He tells my father where he is taking me, to the back of someone's car where they are all taking turns.

"Not this one," my father says.

Slowly the old man shifts his approach, "Okay, forget the girl, okay, we've already got one. You come, come and take a turn, okay, come on . . ."

"No," my father says. My father's arm is across my shoulders. The old man isn't so big anymore, the big man has dissolved, the old man is old and he is whining. My father steers me away from this man, back to the front of the hall. We return to the laughing faces and the three-legged races and, of course, the ball games.

Tales of a Weeping Womb

As a teen and as an adult I have learned many words for female genitalia: cunt, cunny, peachka, putka, vagina, vulva, yoni, and endless euphemisms. Never, outside of family parlance, have I come across the term I first learned, *little bum*.

I've lived as long with my periods as without them, at this point. Although I know they won't be with me forever, I feel some affection for this part of my life. I know that when they are gone for good, I will not say "good riddance," will not feel particularly emancipated, but will look back warmly on that long track of my life when I did have this internal calendar of days, marked by the weeping womb spilling her blood. Menopause can be sometimes harsh, so there may be some relief in my bodymind once I've walked that passage completely.

MENARCHE

The first time was just a belly ache for me, same with the second. I remember excusing myself, leaving my dad, brothers and sisters watching "The Last Spike" on TV, to silently roll around in the kitchen gasping, gather my wits once again and modestly retake my seat in the living room. Later, checking my underwear in the bathroom, there was no evidence of the change I felt in my body. Not yet. I was disappointed, because my friends on other farms had already started. For a few months my self-esteem dipped a bit and I encouraged my body along, hoping to avoid the stigma of being a late-bloomer.

When I first saw the mark, blood in my pants, I was not yet relieved. I was puzzled. I'd been told I would find blood, but what I found looked more like a dark rust, dry and powdery. Eventually my bodymind found her stride and the blood came, dry, fresh, more or less regularly, with or without mild swelling, cramps. Whenever I'm deeply stressed the blood is withheld, which has made for at least one false alarm for almost every fling, affair or one night stand I indulged in.

Puerperal and Blue

The worst periods I ever had followed a spontaneous miscarriage. I was in my late teens, living with other teens in a tiny prairie apartment. The doctor alienated me by calling me a "soft touch," several times, when I went in for a pregnancy test. In his office, I was so focussed on getting medical information that I didn't respond to his name-calling, which is why he had to repeat it a number of times. The moment I stepped out of the office, I understood, and was so enraged that over the days the puerperal fever set in, I refused to go see him. I was hallucinatory for days, on a mattress on the floor, paranoid and otherwise sundered from the everyday world.

I survived, luckily. Each period thereafter brought on a

mini-collapse, with all the symptoms returning, each month a little less incapacitating, until my body had sorted through all the poisons and life returned to normal. In case you're now miscarrying and your doctor's an asshole, I will tell you that you should not have sex while miscarrying. Whether you feel pain or not, put your vulva in the sick room, take care of her yourself with love, affection and nurture, and don't let any dirt or germs get near her.

You're Not Keeping Those In the Bathroom, Are You?

At university I shared a house with some male students who carried a lot of embarrassment, intolerance and shame around female bodies. Shortly after I moved in, financially broke and emotionally on edge, I was asked about my big box of pads, which these liberal-minded young gentlemen had never imagined knocking around with their razors and aftershave. One month, with particularly painful cramps and swelling, and given the vibes I was getting from the men, I ended up flashing back to a scene of violence with my father, his arm suspended over me in malignant threat. Co-ed lifestyles will be much more successful when the separate cutures of girls and boys are acknowledged, and alliance-building becomes the freedom-loving norm instead of pretense.

Bloody Family

My family shared a straightforward, generally positive attitude toward bodily life, and I was not teased or shamed about bleeding, cramping, or fertility. I was raised Catholic, and teased for being both dark and flat-chested, but I was fairly comfortable having my periods and didn't understand girls or women who called it "the curse." In my early twenties, I read Germaine Greer's anti-body literature; although I agreed with much, her rejection of womanly bodies struck me as wrong. I also read more celebratory writings by feminists about menstruation, and to these I responded well. My casual acceptance of my periods grew slightly, as if the blood were a mark of my presence, my identity, an assertion of womanhood. As a family woman, a breeder, a mother, I have found that the absence of blood is as much an expression of womanhood as is its presence. Walking the fertile crescent of pregnancy, birth and nursing, I have been a full woman unaccompanied by the periodic weeping of the womb. I miss about eighteen months of bleeding per child, nursing each child for an average of two years.

Reclaiming Sacred Space

In many traditional sacred practices, women on the rag are asked not to participate in the usual ways. The reasons given vary from cries of "pollution" to fears of "excessive power." It is true that menstruation—moontime—is one of our processes of elimination, harmonizing and cleansing. For both First Nations and European North Americans, the problem is based on a history of the decimation of traditional women's practices and rituals, from the sharing of midwifery skills to whatever rites of passage any particular community of women marked and celebrated. This imbalance—where the larger community continues to ask for a change in relationship, yet the parallel women-only tradition may no longer be in place—has caused women to sometimes rage and feel excluded. Better to rebuild what we have lost, than to throw away what remains of our non-Christian cultural expressions.

Two highlights of having my period, both of which happened when I wasn't having my period, relate to menstruation in the here and now as sacred space, for the community and human life as a whole, but especially for women.

A friend of mine, in response to great pain on a monthly basis, pulled a few women together and led us in a healing ritual specifically focussed on menstruation. At the core/ kore of the ritual, she invited us to put all the lies we had ever been told about our bodies, our periods, our lives into a shoe box. Together we cast them into a fire and watched them burn. We called out in loud voices all the truths we wanted known about our blood, ourselves, our lives. Transforming the lies we'd carried so long into the freedom to affirm and enjoy our selves, reclaiming the rightness of our being in the world as embodied women in this place and time, was a true and deep healing, an essential celebration for us all.

After the miscarriage, it took another seven years and two abortions before I felt safe enough, strong enough and intrigued enough to give childbearing a chance. The diverse feelings of wonder and awe that surrounded this pregnancy process formed the basis of a deep change in who I am. Putting together the idea that my heterosexual activities and my monthly bleeding could somehow combine to ignite a new human form that would gather and grow right inside my body—that this correlation was much more than rumour, lies or outdated information—was a powerful reality check for me.

In living the proof on a daily basis, I reconnected with many aspects of myself previously lost, damaged or buried under duress. I set aside as much of the modern baggage I'd collected as I could, such as sex = pregnancy = abortion; and/or sex = pregnancy = slavery (motherhood); and/or sex = pregnancy = shaming (soft touch, eh?), in order to integrate the primordial reality of what I was experiencing.

The final stage of birthing, as defined by midwives, is delivery of the placenta and other womb-furnishings no longer required by the newly born child. In this first birth, this stage was very long, as my overfull bladder blocked egress for all but the child. The midwife used a narrow tube to drain away the urine. That done, I squatted over a shallow basin, which quickly filled with blood and afterbirth. Gazing into this pool of blood, seeing reflected there a radically altered geography, I was deeply touched. Something irrevocable had happened.

Human and earthy magic. Experiences of embodiment, power and divinity in a Female Aspect. Life force deeper and wilder than any I had recognized or experienced before. Forever after, my pride in my period and innate femaleness has been much less theoretical and political, much more potent, experiential, sensory-based and sacred.

Surrendering a Solitary God

For seven years I and various members of my family and our friends gathered together periodically to investigate and celebrate folk/pagan European holy days. Some called themselves witches, some pagans, some didn't take on any particular labels. Some were quite vigilant and observed phases of the Moon as well as the numerous sun-and-earth-related occasions such as the Solstices—the longest dark and the longest day—and the Equinoxes, transitory moments of balance—Sowing Spring and Harvesting Autumn—and so on. With each year and for each individual, the celebrations varied, but certain common traits were learned and shared. We learned to recognize holy ways and holy days, we learned to peel back the Christian overlay to see what fundamentally remained.

What we had learned so deeply as people raised in a Christian society was obedience to authority outside of ourselves. The antidote was seven years of ritual-making. What we had lost was a sense of Being Regnant, and what we regained was courage, flexibility, the ability to decide, create, design and celebrate our own unique expressions of spirituality, as individuals and as co-operative group members.

My original intention here was to write about the family altar, what remains beyond that period of ritual work, with its home-making centrality, and the various items found on our altars—perhaps to reach some definition of my "religion" or "spirituality" that is more descriptive than "post-Christian." As you will see, that is not what is recorded here at all. What follows is a history, a geography, a biography: a few notes on spirituality and religion.

The impression many have gained in this Christian/misogynist place is that Girl's and Woman's most spiritual role is that of the sacrificial beast on the family altar. Movements by First Nations people to reclaim traditional and healing ways, by Celtic-origins folk to revivify pre-Christian ways, and by women of all kinds to reclaim, revivify and/or recreate devotional practices linked to celebrations of the Divine Female in some of Her limitless Forms, are all signs of an awakening of power after just a few centuries of the New Dark Ages.

Canada is in many ways a dispirited place. How it came to be that way is a story of cultural domination and racism of the worst kind, of exactly the same kind we read about in the newspapers and schoolbooks about other groups, other times, other places. Dominant forces in Canadian society, as expressed through the laws and actions of Canadians at every level of community, from federal down to the most dinky little municipal place possible, have a history just as blinkered, greedy and righteously self-serving as the more famed examples of rotten communities elsewhere in the world. It has been only one hundred and fifty years since slavery was outlawed in Canada. The impression made on the generations subsequent to the change in laws, wherein Canada became for a time safe haven for African-American refugees from the U.S., has almost obliterated the fact that for at least a hundred and fifty years before that, slavery was fine and dandy.

Within the dominant, western European groups, there has been a long struggle between those seeking separation of church and state, and those pulling the other way. Given that representatives of church have long and often been drawn from the same families as representatives of state— the legal, business, academic and medical establishments— it is no big surprise that, formally or informally, co-operation between these various forces has more often than not been the rule. While white governments enacted a long series of laws and practices that economically debilitated and paralyzed the majority of First Nations communities, church representatives actively worked to interrupt and undermine the inner fibre of First Nations social and sacred integrity.

On the recommendation of churchmen, no doubt, governments in Canada outlawed most traditional First Nations social, religious and healing practices, while pouring much money into the churches for their front-line work as cultural combat forces. The Sun Dance and the Potlatch are two western practices only recently returning from the secrecy imposed by legal banning. For most of this century, First Nations communities were required by law to send their children to residential schools for ten months of the year. As resistance by the communities persisted, the options were closed down: parents who refused to give their children up for ten months of each year were visited by government representatives who, with full legal backing, stole the children outright, removing them to white, Christian families and communities. Foster and adoption systems—supposedly intended as supports to children, families and communities—were used to depopulate First Nations communities and to demoralize First Nations people at every level. Into the present time, Inuit women who choose to birth in traditional ways must go into hiding in order to escape the "assistance" of medical representatives of Canada's southern white society, who will otherwise force them into small planes to be carried south to hospitals, for the medically controlled, interventionist-style births this society deems to be normal.

In spite of their dominant hold on this and many other societies, Christians persist in nurturing their young on tales of the repression and oppression of Christians. These tales are very old indeed, if not convenient fabrications twisted together through the centuries of church control, to instil fierce pride of a fearful, defensive kind alongside the expansive righteousness that characterizes the group mind of this community. As traditional and mainstream churches slowly lose popularity, fundamentalist and charismatic groups thrive, teaching more of the same.

As a church-going girl, I was led to fear Jews and, at the same time, to see them and Israel as very ancient, rather than modern, current and co-existent with me. In the same way, my schooling in Catholic and public schools led me to both fear and dismiss First Nations people, as opposed to recognizing them both around and within me. In Catholic school, I was given the distinct impression that there were only two kinds of people in all the world: Catholics and Protestants. As a Catholic, I was right to fear the power and hostility of Protestant people, not only in a general societal way, but as concretely as to require vigilance on the way home from school. The internal coherence of this information structure was not good, as the endless pool of heathen to be converted in every era was not seen as Protestant, nor, of course, as Catholic. As my sense of the world expanded, my difficulty in placing Hinduism, Islam, the Potlatch and witchcraft into this narrow context began to truly boggle my mind. I had to give up this tidy organizational tool, and look elsewhere for a framework to integrate my life experiences, to assist me in formulating a sensible, workable worldview.

The disease between Catholics and Protestants was not, of course, the simple concoction of paranoid minds. The persecution of the Métis and other francophone Canadians, predominantly Catholic, at the hands of the Protestan ruling class, has left resentments that are still being played out, religious differences now perhaps overshadowed by differences of language, region and race. I clearly remember playing a game on the way home from Catholic school, on the west coast, pointing into the trees and shouting, *Look out, it's the FLQ!*[1] Negotiations between anglophones and francophones, subsumed into negotiations between Canada and Quebec, have gone on, gathering sophistication and a peer quality, throughout my lifetime. The pinnacle of that process was the dream of a gentleman's deal to define the nation of Canada as west European, at Meech Lake, a blinkered vision burst with the feather-wielding, quietly potent assertion of First Nations presence, in the person of Manitoba MLA Elijah Harper. The lesson was spelled out in the Oka conflict, where race, language, power and religious permutations revealed, to those paying attention, the complexities we're dealing with. The lessons were underlined repeatedly in the form of roadblocks, diverted rivers and court challenges across the regions.

In English Canada, the dominant forces seem to have a compulsion for tidiness that joins with the empowered perversity and repressive response to non-Christian ways and deities. Many people who come here from elsewhere notice an emptiness to our streets, a lack of joy. There are no vendors on the streets except in tightly controlled circumstances. There are few parades of people celebrating community of any sort, the closest approximations being the motorized parades of things (with a few vestigal humans attached) like the Santa Claus and Antique Car parades, and the protest marches that occasionally grace the larger cities, gathering people around issues of dissatisfaction and the need for Change in Her many guises. The Christian dissatisfaction with what is, and the unwillingness to celebrate what is—except in a depressive, keep-on-slugging frame of mind —has entirely permeated the society. Statistics on "the unemployed" are batted around on a daily basis, along with a puritanical disdain of the shiftless and the lazy. Yet the legislative stranglehold on individual, spontaneous economic activity remains unquestioned, and the condemnation of "subsistence" modes of living continues to be propagated in schools and via the media. Spirituality itself is pushed behind doors that are only in some cases recognizable as places of worship.

In response to this dispiritedness, individuals of many groups are casting around for more nourishing expressions of the sacred, seeking to heal and revivify ourselves, our communities and our relationship with the nonhuman world.

Within the mainstream, there are forces of change as well, the result of decades of cross-cultural infusions. Tai chi, martial arts, yoga, meditation, ayurvedha, acupuncture and applications of Taoist and other Asian philosophies are making inroads into both the Canadian marketplace and the collective mind.

When I first looked up the term "Taoist" in a library reference book, I was disappointed to read that it was a "dead religion." Subsequently an explosion of English-language publishing in the realm of Taoism and Tao-influenced thinking has occurred. The centuries-old communities of Asian North Americans are joined by new waves of immigrants, and at the same time by a surge of renewed interest in non-European ways by a variety of North American seekers. This invasion of the privacy of heretofore subjugated and isolated communities continues to have repercussions. For instance, Canadian Chinese communities grapple with a sudden diversification, influx of new money and opinion, and a great deal more exposure to, and requests for input from, Euro-Canadians. Old and new families mix with some dissension, as the generations of oppression and persecution, influence and assimilation sometimes contrast sharply with the differing impact of recent history on newly arriving people from China, Japan, India and other Asian societies. At the same time, a cultural renascence, renaissance, is at hand, expressed religiously, artistically and economically, visible both within the various "Chinatowns" and throughout the dominant/mainstream/public spheres.

Few Euro-Canadians recognize the missionary aspect of tai chi, yoga and martial arts instruction, ayurvedha, acupressure, acupuncture and Chinese herbal medical alternatives, Japanese Zen aesthetics — yet each of these additions to our cultural repetoire for survival grows out of fully developed cosmological, philosophical, religious and medical systems that are definitely not Christian. Just as Christian missionary efforts continue to offer western European-style education, medicine, political influence and money in exchange for a toe-hold on the bodyminds of Asian people overseas, North Americans are learning alternative ways of being in the world, and of perceiving the world, without leaving home. The most impressive religious building in the area where I currently live, and the most beautiful building of any kind in this area, is Buddhist. The Quan Yin Tan, or temple, is vibrantly ornate and richly decorous in a traditional Chinese way.

There have been gathering forces within the various Christian communities as well, resulting in wholesale re-evaluations of the images of God, metaphors for God, ways of worshipping God, with surges toward inclusivity meeting up with opposing surges of fundamentalist, patriarchal re-assertion. I have some compassion for the women and men who attempt to revive Christianity and make it more wholesome. I have in the past struggled to make my Christian training cohere with my need for a safe spiritual place of nurture and strength in my life.

Being Catholic, I was raised with images of the Divine and Holy Female, in the forms of a God-Mother and numerous martyrs and saints, perverted by the bloodymindedness and misogyny of church traditions, but present nonetheless. Just as the public domain led me to believe I could grow up to be a mother, nurse, secretary or teacher, the Catholic domain expanded my options. If you are unimaginative and blessed, you can bring new little babies to Jesus as wife-mother. If you like to travel, be a missionary. Do you want to tend the poor, the ignorant, the sick? Become a Bride of Christ, be a nun. For the very ambitious (although you cannot choose this, you can pray for the honour), there are the sacred roles of martyr and saint to strive and die for.

Throughout my fundamental training, I was given the impression there was space for me. Things only became really complicated when I began to evaluate the possibilities, tried to think them through, especially in combination with the feminist and working-class rebelliousness I was also learning. As one of six sequential sisters, my earliest years were quite female-dominant. We routinely traded challenges like, "So Who Are You? Queen of the World?" "Oh yeah, Queen of the Universe, we hear and obey!" The combined influence of Roman Catholic Mary, British Monarch Elizabeth, Stay-At-Home Mother Lorraine and Visiting-Often Grandmother Marie-Louise, within a family context of six girl children very close in age indeed, created the initial impression that being female was both normal and okay. Reaching the age of reason and schooling, from my seventh year on, I was roundly disabused of that notion.

I understand that Christianity is not a monolith and that permutations of Christianity, tempered by the traditional and innovative thoughts and expressions of different individuals and communities around the world, can be more or less biophilic, more or less healthy for individuals and communities of practitioners. Yet my experience, first as a

Christian and then as a post-Christian outsider, is of course more palpable to me and more persuasive. When I read now in Canadian newspapers of Christian women calling on Sophia, and Christian men calling it heresy, I shake my head in sad wonderment. What are those women doing in there? Why don't they come out here, step away?

Most information in English, French, or Spanish, secular or otherwise, is available only through the cultural warp of Christian domination. Definitions of sacred space, religion, worship, deity, spirituality, reality, humanity, all are subject to the deformative, biophobic stance of the dominant Christians. The grip of that perspective is not solely on self-identified Christians. The grip is pervasive, affecting nondominant groups of every possible religious and cultural tradition, as attempts are made to forge coherence among the disparate and conflicting aspects of cultures, languages, societies and communities within a Christian-dominant context. One example is the tendency among Euro-North American feminists today to speak about the Goddess and/or Goddesses in the past tense; like Jewish people, and First Nations people, the Goddess is and always has been alive and kicking, both elsewhere in the world and here today.

For women raised within the confines of the Christian mainstream, it is possible to live out our entire lives without finding even a taste of the sacred within ourselves, much less represented to us by others from the outside. Western art, so thoroughly compromised by and entangled with Christianity, fails entirely to celebrate what is unique about women as women, and overexposes our nakedness along with fruits, vegetables, farmlands and animals felled by the hunt, all presented with the presumption of male audience, sentience and dominance. Religious themes celebrate suffering, death and resurrection; women's roles are those of the mourning, the damned and, very occasionally, the mother, sometimes breastfeeding, never birthing.

I distinctly recall the impact, at the age of twenty-one, of my visit to the Toronto Art Gallery, viewing for the first time a series of Japanese prints that included scenes of women at the baths. A flush of embarrassment and heat, widening of eyes and first pulling away, then surreptitiously leaning in for a closer look. In all my years I had rarely seen a vulva depicted, and in the few depictions I'd come across in galleries and on alley walls, they were generally presented in the shape of the letter *Y*, very occasionally the letter *O*. The letter *O* was beyond me, at that point, though I could recreate the shape of the letter *Y* in myself by vigorously clenching my pelvis and thighs. In the absence of other information, I reluctantly accepted this as normal.

The more relaxed, anatomically correct and revolutionary representation of a vulva in the shape of a *W* blew me away. Later viewings of Judy Chicago's *The Dinner Party*, works of other feminist artists in magazines and studios, and later again several installments of Chicago et al.'s *The Birth Project*, were like food for the hungry, for me and many thousands of others. The importance of the Japanese prints was not only that I saw them first but that they were old, representing to me for the first time an alternative human history.

I read recently about a Japanese village being mocked and shamed into giving up its traditional parade featuring a giant phallus carried through the streets. The article mentioned as an aside that a nearby village, that had similarly paraded a giant vulva since time out of mind, had earlier been mocked and shamed into abandoning its practice. This seems to me to be the influence of Christian denial of human reality, and it pains me.

I have also read recently that childbirth did not appear in Western artistic representation for a period of some two thousand years. Excepting the few medical prints of men reaching inside women's voluminous skirts, this absence of imagery carried forward into the 1930s, to be finally filled by Mestiza artist Frida Kahlo, painting in Mexico, and other artists. It is my guess that throughout this silent period, images of women's realities, of women's acts of Creation and of birthing, and of the Divine Female, were created, maintained and destroyed over and over. Consider the possibilities for us all, as girls, women, boys and men, of growing up in a place where the female aspects of and expressions of human and sacred life are marked by their presence, as opposed to their absence.

Imagine a place where Goddess is revered not only as God-Mother, but as Mother-God, as Grandmother, Queen, Warrior and Empress; as Divine Creater, Ruler, Succour and Destroyer; as Spider, Coyote, Hippopotamus, Lioness, Snake and Toad; as Earth, Ocean, Wind, River, Underworld and Heaven. These places exist, obscured and occluded by Christianization, yet open to and much older than the gaze of any human person alive today.

Even within a male dominant purview, consider the difference between gazing each day of your life on the relaxed visage of a meditating golden Buddha, and a bleeding, agonized or despondent, crucified Christ. The health and integrity of any bodymind, the perceptions of what is usual, possible and probable, must differ immensely.

There are qualitative differences inherent in growing up in a dispirited, tidy place like the mainstream of Christian-Canada, and a place where spiritual and religious expression is out front, taken to the kitchen, to the forest, to the meadow, to the streets, whether the expressive community exists within the realm of Canada or some place else in the world. These disparities are immeasurable, yet must somehow be brought onto the scale of global realities.

In Taiwan, a place with many troubles of its own, small altars appear on the streets at regular intervals, outside businesses, apartment buildings and temples alike. A majority of shops maintain altars large or small on the premises, an integrated part of daily life. Obvious places of worship proliferate, from tiny temples the size of a kiosk, and large statues of Ma Tsu, Kuan Yin or Buddha accompanied by altars an incense burners in public parks, to huge, sprawling temple and monastery complexes stretching across the mountainsides and other landscapes of the country. Community religious expressions in the forms of parades and other gatherings are visible to the most ignorant observer, such as myself, on a regular basis.

Chinese popular religion, with its inclusive response to new dieties and new forms of worship, is almost impossible to define by western Christian standards. One anthropological observer, Margery Wolfe, grappled with the fact that the family altar is kept in a place where work is done, gatherings happen and children play. Rather than making the leap to understanding that work, play, community and children are sacred, she left her observation hanging uncomfortably, puzzled by the sacred object so commonly and inexplicably positioned in an obviously secular space.[2]

In Canada, First Nations people imprisoned by the state still have regular struggles in the realm of religious integrity. Prison staff remove medicine bundles and pouches, disrespecting, disregarding, and/or simply being *unable to perceive* the healing, the enspiriting role of these bundles. Sweats, healing circles and use of medicines in prisons are a privilege, easily revoked.

Mainstream Canada, like so many "First World" countries, heir to so many centuries of Christian permeation and struggle, is denatured and dispirited to a point of unholy, unwholesome blindness, from the largest grouping to the most isolated individual unit/person. The endless array of problems that result range from the imposition of a European-Christian monoculture and cultural/racial intolerance on the one hand, to a starved, even vampirical approach to other ways and other cultures on the other.[3]

Taiwanese history parallels the Canadian experience in many ways, particularly that of French Canada and the Québécois. Aboriginal nations have co-existed with, warred with and been legislated almost out of existence by dominant, immigrant populations whose primary contemporary interest in the Taiwanese First Nations is as tourist-oriented cash commodities. A second foreign power (the Japanese) moved in for fifty years, only to be supplanted by a third (the Mainlanders). Taiwan is now home to about the same number of people as Canada, on a land base about the size of Vancouver Island. The complex status of the province/country has required a fostering of economic, artistic, scientific and other ties with other countries, while politically Taiwan remains an outsider, with formal relations only to other outsider countries like South Africa, Israel and Nicaragua.

Taiwan has been described to me as a Buddhist country, but what is obvious to this visitor's eye is the diversity of religious expression, with Ma Tsu, Goddess of the Sea, being perhaps as widely acclaimed as the Buddha, and worshipped alongside Buddhist, Taoist and other popular Chinese deities. The current ruling class was assisted into position by a timely though perhaps superficial conversion to Christianity, the price of support of American firepower. The majority of western foreigners in Taiwan are Christian missionaries and businessmen. The student subculture of North American seekers after non-American ways is, to some extent, undercut by their work as teachers of English, inadvertent tools and assistants to the mass exportation of Christian American culture.

Political suppression in Taiwan today hinges on the still insecure grip of the ruling class now attempting to take on the cloak of popular democracy; on the terror of invasion by the Mainland rendering any talk of independence radical and suspect; and on the derogation of cultures different from the dominant, Chinese, one. It is possible for a North American to go to Taiwan to meet the Goddess, but it is not possible to go to Taiwan and find Utopia, or a respectful response by an immigrant nation to Aboriginal peoples and cultures.

Many people in Canada have strong ties to their traditional cultures. As many again do not, by reason of separation from their homeplaces and enforced ignorance, or repeated intermarriages resulting in multiracial people with only the dominant norm for guidance, or any of the other forces in social history that have the common impacts of erasure, forgetting. The need is great, for every person and on every level, to reclaim the sacred in ourselves, in our surroundings and in our lives. Whether a practice is very old or very new does make a difference, but in the end what is important is the re-animation of ourselves, our relationships, our communities, a resurgence of not only the Divine Female but of the unlimited recognition of divinity and the sacred in our worlds, in all our relations.

There is a vast psychological rift between those who grow up in a homeplace, where each plant, tree, animal, mountain, valley, river, shore, person and family has a history, an identity, a role to play in life and an acknowledged sacredness, and those who grow up in an away place, any away place at all, where old names are applied to new surroundings, where stories do not fit and are soon adapted or forgotten, where the present place has been dug under and made over to resemble the away place that was home, where the sense of dislocation, uneasiness, strangeness lingers on even after many generations.

A delicate sense of cultural difference is essential to

move forward out of that hurt, paralyzed position that modern life and a Christian upbringing has abandoned so many of us to. Tearing down a worldview is risky business, but there is information available, and both human and divine help abounds. Giving up Original Sin for Original Face, surrendering a solitary, punitive God and the warring factions of self for the diversity of juicy, lively, convivial (and angry and punitive) Goddesses, Gods, Immortals and Spirit-Forces extant, is worthy of the risk. It is in fact a surrender into What You Once Knew, resynchronization, grounding and centring, a re-harmonization of self and world the way you once were, way back, to begin with.

NOTES

1 Front de Libération du Québec, a revolutionary group advocating the independence of Québec, founded in the early 1960s.
2 A male Taiwanese anthropologist dismissed Wolfe's work as the "projections" of a western white woman observer. Taiwanese anthropologist and feminist Elaine Tsui referred in a seminar to Wolfe's *Women and the Family in Rural Taiwan* as "the bible."
3 See Beth Brant, "Anodynes and Amulets," *Writing As Witness* (Toronto: The Women's Press, 1994), for an uncompromising analysis of the use of fragments of Indigenous cultures by New Age religionists.

Tale of Three Jingles

When a young child, or any relaxed person, learns a new song, there is often a process of playing with the words and melody before the "true" version sets. Some of these variations can be more true and/or more beautiful than the original. On the other end of the spectrum, a person who knows a song only too well and is put in the position of singing it informally, endlessly, day and night—a situation many an adult friend of young children has found themselves in—will again begin to subvert and change the original, sometimes merely out of boredom and in a spirit of either rebellion or free play, and sometimes as a way of bringing the song in, to more fully express the singer's own reality. Here I present three traditional Euro-North American children's songs, as revamped by my children and/or myself.

BLACK SHEEP

Learning "Baa Baa Black Sheep" proved trying for my young son, there were so many words. His musical aesthetic too was as much formed by the Talking Heads and The

Pretenders as by orally passed, traditional tunes. Being a city dweller, the mercantile relationship suggested between singer and beast was obscure for him. In the absorbent way that children have, he seemed to present me with a family anthem when he devised and perfected this song, sung with a rocking beat:

> Black sheep everywhere
> Black sheep everywhere
> Black sheep everywhere
> Yeah, yeah, yeah

Each of the first three lines drops a tone, and each "yeah" rises a tone. It's punchy. I once had the pleasure of teaching this song at a women's workshop, sharing it with about a hundred other "black sheep." It seems to capture the sense that most of us in this society have, at least most of us women and children, of being not quite right somehow.

SUBVERTING MACDONALD

Growing up in Winnipeg, one of the delights of my existence was to visit my aunt's farm. She and her husband had a garden, and meat and dairy cattle, horses, chickens, geese and pigs, fields of grain and pasture and wooded lots with livestock trails winding between poplar trees and abandoned cars and tractors. Farming being as it is, my uncle generally had to work for cash in other places. My aunt was usually the full-time farmer, assisted by her husband and children.

As a young mother singing "Old MacDonald Had a Farm" over and over and over, I had plenty of opportunity to think and remember about farms and farmers, and my aunt, and farm women generally. I began to rebel against this endless listing of some phantom male farmer's living possessions. Much to my child's surprise, one day I sang out:

Old MacDonald had a baby, ee-i-ee-i-oh!
With a wah wah here, a wah wah there,
Here a wah, there a wah, everywhere a wah wah!
Old MacDonald had a baby, ee-i-ee-i-oh!

I became quite attached to the idea of Old MacDonald having a baby, and eventually devised a storybook text based on the idea (*Ma MacDonald*, Women's Press, 1993). I drew upon my own experience of giving birth at home to describe a completely nonmedical birth experience. In turning the jingle into a tale that would be shared by adults, often new parents, and children, I wanted to provide a positive view of childbirth, to give younger children a sense of what happens when their mothers give birth, without arousing fear. I also wanted to reassure the adults and to celebrate birth: given how widespread childbirth is, it is grossly underrepresented in North American culture/society. Even within feminist circles, NRTS (new reproductive technologies) get lots more attention than the tried and true Vulva. Given the rage the medical patriarchs have been in for the last few centuries, it is a rare resource indeed that is able to separate the fear-mongering from the potent gift; thus the child's tale becomes feminist subversion.

MacDonald and her nine-year-old daughter Mary have prepared for a homebirth, yet when the moment of labour arrives they are in the midst of farm chores, far from the house. As MacDonald finds a comfortable spot to give birth, Mary runs back to the house to bring the sort of pre-pared materials that present-day homebirth attendants require: sterile linens in a paper bag, items for cutting and tying the cord, boiled water for washing up. A very quick labour and birth are portrayed, with no complications what-soever. MacDonald is an experienced mother, as an inexpe-rienced character might lead to a totally different story. This woman, though caught unaware by the onset of labour, has no qualms about delivering her own baby.

Ma MacDonald is a tribute to farm girls and women, and a way to share an adventure where the challenge is met with high energy on the part of all participants. An important aspect of the story is the demonstrated ability of both mother and daughter to remain competent and aware while caught up in highly charged events. Too frequently we are given the message that emotionality and excitement lead to disaster and stupidity, particularly so for girls and women. I'm interested in promoting the view that responding appropriately to challenging situations doesn't interfere with excitement in the least, and in fact, adds pride of accom-plishment to the adventure.

The main message is that birth is a natural life process and worthy of our attention. The importance of sharing this reality cannot be emphasized enough. Most children of recent generations are hyper-aware of violence and death, via television, books and life, and are under-informed of positive, living realities. They are told little about birth, which is considered not a fit subject for young people. Our origins, our roots are obscured.

Most women who give birth wander off one or two at a time, into a realm still very much controlled by the patriarchy. The patriarchy, in this case, are the men and women programmed through an intensive medical education that leaves most of them gasping, a huge charge of terror attached to their understanding of childbirth. The simplicity and power of birth is distorted, even demonized, through the repetitive witnessing of the horrific consequences of systemic interventionist practices and procedures. Women know that birth is a life and death situation. Our chances are best when we go with life, rather than struggle against it. The inhibitions imposed by the medical establishment's dehumanized approach to childbearing, the dislocation of authority from childbearing women to medical staff, substantially weakens a woman's ability to rise and change and thrive through the birthing process. The resurgence of midwifery and home-births exists within this context, expressive of the need and desire to reclaim this decisive, formative and fundamental aspect of our lives.

The concluding scene in *Ma MacDonald* shows Mary, her mother and the baby surrounded by others, drawn together to celebrate the birth, signifying family and community support. This kind of recognition is invaluable for mothers of young children, who too often feel dropped out of acceptable society. The integrity of the community depends upon its ability to acknowledge, to encompass and ensconce all of its members.

My favourite part of all this is how predictive the tale turned out to be. I developed the manuscript version while pregnant with my second child; the daughter in the story was named for my midwife, Mary Sullivan. In the story, the child Mary runs back to the house to get the supplies and returns to find MacDonald sitting with the baby, a boy, in her arms. The evening before I gave birth, midwife Mary had supper at our place, and as she left the mild cramping I'd had off and on for a week started up again. By the time we called her back, a very quick labour was in progress and she arrived to find me sitting with a naked new infant in my arms.

ROCK

rock-
a-bye baby
on the tree top

when the winds blow
the cradle
will rock

if the bough breaks
the cradle
may fall

but I'll catch
my baby
cradle

and all

rock-
a-bye babies
on the tree top

when the wind blows
the cradles
may rock

if the boughs break
the cradles
may fall

but I'll catch my babies
cradles
and

all

rock

This revision of "Rock-a-bye Baby" grew organically out of my parenting of my first child. My own childhood was fraught with violence, and all the past seemed to come up for review during the first few years after his birth. Learning to control and direct my sometimes violent temper, to reach out for assistance instead of repeating the spiral of child abuse, and to forgive myself for being a real woman instead of the ideal font of nurture my child so obviously deserved, formed the greater part of my task in learning to mother.

Given the circumstances, it was painful in the good times to croon the traditional, and threatening, "down will come baby, cradle and all . . ." over and over. The number of words I changed are few, yet the entire feeling of the song is shifted. "The winds" for me are the hassles of life — poverty and welfare workers, flashbacks to unhappy times and feelings of inadequacy, intense feelings of rage and grief that sometimes overwhelm. With those things acknowledged, the threat of abandonment or actual dropping of the child can be set aside, and the promise, which strengthens with repetition, can be made: "I'll catch my baby," I will catch you, I will ensure your safety as best I can. "Rock" performs as a mantra or healing affirmation in the struggle to break the chain of child abuse, neglect and abandonment, by acknowledging the struggle while remaining grounded in moments of peace, the relief of good times, and the central/potential goodheartedness of the family connection.

Another layer to the song is the acknowledgement of feelings of displacement for an older child, with a new baby born into the household. By always singing the song twice, once in the singular (baby) and once in the plural (babies), the promise is made to remember both, to catch both the new and the already-present "baby." The shift that occurs as a child grows out of infancy and beyond toddlerhood, particularly if there is a new baby on the scene, can be quite dramatic. The shine has come off. Once-doting relatives and friends can become much less attentive, less affectionate and tolerant of the older child. This can be a very real loss, hard for both the growing child and those adults clos-est in, observing the change. It is a relief to be reassured that you are still a precious and valuable human presence.

The song begins and ends with the word "rock," refer-ring both to the hard, barren times, and to bedrock, the foundation that adults provide the children around them to grow on and against, the ground of being. It also evokes modern musical forms, the sense of breaking away from old forms and traditions and creating new ones that fit and express the new wave of humanity more perfectly. As a feminist mother and the daughter of a feminist mother, it is important to me not to throw out the baby with the bath water: my mother's response to her oppression as a mother was to leave and to re-connect with her children years later. I am usually optimistic that, for me today, other solutions can be found.

I have found that singing "Rock" to adults, after reading poetry about the perils of my own childhood — the overt violence, the mind-bending denial of Native heritage, the prohibitions against connecting to any wider community — has a sometimes profound effect. There is something hope-ful in its promise, the optimism that in fact someone can, and someone will, "catch [the] babies, cradles and all."

Song is a whole body, whole mind activity that joins and heals us. To all black sheep everywhere, I offer these three jingles as alternative lullabies.

Something Impressive[1]

We are speaking today about issues of murder and menace, and the way these things come to present themselves through our writings. I write poetry and nonfiction. In preparing for this talk, I became anxious, somehow shifted the title around from "Imagining Murder and Menace" to "Imagining Murder and Mayhem." The breakthrough came when I realized that I can leave the mayhem aside, for now.

So. Something impressive. When I am gazing at the moon with pen in hand, what moves me? Awaiting the precipitation of poetic expression, what comes to me is a kind of constellation struck, a few words from all the words I've ever heard, a few images from all the things I've seen or dreamed, a few feelings or sensations that form the vehicle, the motivation, the passion that drives the eclectic little bits into coherence. They say, *write what you know.* Of course, that is inevitable.

I have a few thoughts to share on life and death. Murder and menace are tools of control, a grand behaviour modification scheme to disempower children, to tear children away from our natural power, and to maintain that disempowered state among poor people, among women, among Aboriginal people, among whatever groups it is most necessary and convenient for a dominant social group to keep down. If murder is a crime of passion, it is expressive of a kind of passion carefully cultivated through oppressive societies.

Revolution is not the usual response. Most common is the internalizing and reenactment and contagion of murder and menace within and between oppressed people. Few children murder our parents. Few women murder men. More often women and children and men murder ourselves, call it suicide, and more often still we simply live as small as we can, take up as little space as we possibly can, co-operate as well as we possibly can and try to steal away a little self-esteem, a little happiness, a little pleasure, a tiny bit of fulfillment. Within that small space we lash out, wounding the child next to us, the fools who see something worth loving in us, the unfortunate ones near at hand who simply don't scare us.

Murder in my life has been threefold. Something promised to me often and a few times nearly delivered. Something I use imaginatively to relieve the pain of having been overpowered. Something I have used sparingly to clear the way for my own life's progress.

Something impressive.

Menace. Menace is contagious, something impressed upon me by television, radio, books, film, by men on the streets, by women. Brooding anger. Seething rage. An accumulation of ugliness about to be unleashed indiscriminately. The promise of hurt and destruction.

Menace is an aspect of culture that has walked out of my own mouth, my eyes, my bodymind, and inscribed itself upon my children and my sisters and my lovers. Like most people, I am a great coward. I rarely menace those who have menaced me. I simply fall apart under duress, and menace is re-created through me to bind the wings of a new generation.

Something impressive. I write what I know. Here is a story about a Half-breed man, his children and his white friends. The men are presented with a series of dilemmas; notice the elegant solutions they find for themselves.

Manitoba Pastoral[2]

In a peculiar way, he favoured her.
She got to hold the chickens
while he cut off their heads.
While I cooked and washed dishes,
she dragged the honey bucket to the bush;
it was heavy as she was.
When he worked at the mushroom farm,
she had to wash his clothes out by hand, night
after night, getting the shit out.

One summer we went to a barbecue
held by a neighbour, to honour his mother.
She arrived before we did, in tears
and bruises because her boyfriend
couldn't tolerate her being honoured
in any way. Her son was enraged.
A little guy, he started drinking right away
singing "Hit the Road, Jack" over and over;
Jack was the boyfriend's name.

After we had arrived and once
the guys were sufficiently tanked up
he said Okay, let's go, we're gonna kill
the motherfucker. The men
piled into trucks and started driving
away. My father grabbed my sister
said, They're going to kill a man. You have to
come with me. We have to stop them. Off she went,
and they all ended up at our farm,
gang-raping my sister. The rest of us
women and children
passing time
watching the sun go down
waiting
for the men.

Where are the women in this story? One is lying on her daughter-in-law's bed, sobbing; one left years ago, finding the situation intolerable, leaving her children. Where are the others? Certainly not forming a ring of bodies around the girl about to be sacrificed.

I am emphasizing children because all of us, women and men, poor and rich, from every cultural group and enclave across the earth, all of us begin as infants and become children. The older children and the adults around train us into all aspects of culture, all aspects of the uses and abuses of power. If your parents are like mine, they model powerlessness and despair and menace and hatred turned against one's own kind.

Impressive.

Of course, there is and there always has been resistance. None of us steps out of the womb eager to participate in menace, in murder, and our histories of resistance, of preservation and of pride need to be spoken, shared, celebrated. I am very interested in taking part in courageous collaborations, a conspiracy of healing.

I share my tales of life and death, of murder and menace always with the clear motivation of telling the truth, of acknowledging what is, in order to develop clear strategies together for changing what is, for changing what we are teaching our children, and for changing the lives we presently lead into a true celebration of our full human powers and the Great Spirit, the great beauty and possibilities of life on this earth.

They say that men rule over death and women rule birth, that women create life while men destroy it. This is not the case. Women are adults. We have executive power over life and death. Through abortion, infanticide, beating our children to death, through abandonment, through suicide, through murder, we create death. Through our painful participation in a life that does not celebrate our fullness, through teaching others that this small, imbalanced piece of reality is "just the way it is," through acting out our rage and despair privately, we participate in the destruction of life. We re-create death. By taking the easy way, and using menace as a way to curb the behaviour of others as it was used to inhibit us, we participate fully.

Women hold executive power over life and death. That's impressive.

Birth is a life and death situation. I once had a miscarriage, as a teenager, came down with childbed fever, and nearly died. Twice I have become pregnant and aborted the child because I was not yet in a position where I could bring a new person into the world without either killing them or killing myself, given the bundle of pain that I was, given the utter lack of resources available to me. Three times I have given birth at home with my partner, my sisters, my midwives, and been a channel for the tremendous power of new life coming through onto this earth, experienced humanity re-creating itself and been awed, the spark of life sparkling and glittering in my arms.

What is lacking in the dominant western societies is a true and deep appreciation, a true and deep celebration of birth and of life. Murder and menace are a part of what is. So is the re-creation of life, the contemplation of new humans who arrive with the full expectation of support, respect, freedom, connection, space and assistance, who arrive with full eagerness to experience self and the wide world we have tumbled into.

NOTES

1 Panel presentation, "Imagining Murder and Menace," Sixth International Feminist Book Fair, Melbourne, Australia, 29 July 1994.
2 *My Grass Cradle* (Vancouver: Press Gang Publishers, 1992).

Among the Stones[1]

Each time I sit down to set down a few words on this topic, I find myself walking, in fantasy, along a path that winds through the rainforest on the west coast of Canada. Running beside this path under the trees is a creekbed of pale granitic stones, small and innumerable. Between these stones there weaves a flow of fresh cold water, down from some mountainous beginning, rushing for the lowlands. As I walk, something attracts me to the creekbed. I leave the path and hunker down in a half-squat, among the stones. Whatever it is that called to me is found. I pick it up, and hold it in my two hands.

Another story. This is the tale of one precious moment in the birth of my firstborn child. Giving birth, especially for the first time, can be a tremendous experience. I give birth at home. By the time I'd figured out how to arrange myself to allow for this passage of child out of woman, many hours of labour had passed. This particular child was both curious and patient. As his head emerged from my vulva, he opened his eyes wide. He paused, like that, nose, mouth, neck, body and gender still unrevealed, and spoke his first words. I call them his "words of parting/greeting."

They sounded very cheerful, and also, like a question.

I believe that voice is inherent. Each and every living being, including the rocks, the wind, the sea, has voice. What it means to have voice is to have a capacity for story, a capacity for song, a capacity for the expression of self whether that self-expression comes across wordlessly or with words, embodied or without body, among the people or far off from the people and alone.

I'm thinking about the soft bodies[2] that we are, and how absorbent we are, gathering in the voices around us and digesting them. As with food, we incorporate some of our impressions and they become the fibres of our flesh, cells of our blood, granules of bone. We eliminate what we don't need, can't use, don't want. What is traumatic is the kind of impression that we cannot digest easily, it gets stuck in our craw, something too big for us to break down into useable parts. As we grow wider and wiser and bigger, we can take on some of those pearls, carried for decades. Making use of resources inside and outside ourselves, we can eliminate the poisons we may have generated or collected, smooth the ragged places, find the particular way to arrange ourselves that will allow the passage of what is inside moving outside, into the world.

People are porous. We are organized structures both as individuals and at every other level, and we are intimately connected to every other element and every other presence and every other absence in the world. In our least powerful moments, as in our most powerful moments, we are connected. In our absences as well as in our presences, we have an influence, an impact on the rest of the world.

Here is a poem from my first collection, in which I focussed back onto a very silent time in my life.

flatland summer[3]

she sat there eating spiders
lamely off the walls
of inner tensions   pushing sliding
pulling taut and hang-
gliding through air
crunchy spiders
having nothing else to do
when the weeds
grow high around the porch
and the wind files in
from the old road pushing
at the house
solidly still   solidly still   the
elemental walls they
are outside and in   they can be
still and hot   they can be
cool and dim   cool and dim
and the echoes of the silence
running soft and low within
her empty head
crowded head
eyes of fullness

Now here is a related poem, very short, written perhaps a decade later.

Eating flowers
is better
than eating spiders.

Children frown
showing me
my face.

Many of us, particularly those of us who live in urban areas, or become addicted to media, take in such a barrage of impressions that it becomes difficult to express enough to maintain ourselves in a balanced state. More to the point, the vast majority of us are in one way or another silenced, and shut down, forces of intimidation frightening us away from our inherent, expressive powers.

Writing, in itself, is simply marks on a page. Whatever tone we take, whatever genre we use, whatever forms our writings take, it is ourselves as soft bodies, as porous people in the world, as intimately bound up with all parts of time and space and life that is making use of marks on a page to mark our passage.

Writing is one ritualized structure for processing the ongoing contact and intimacy we have with the rest of the world.

Here is another poem, and another story drawn from that first birthing experience. Fifty hours was the length of that labour, twenty-five years my age at the time.

Wrenching Life from the Ghosts[4]

o ghosts and demons
for fifty hours
i held you at bay
i held you at bay
for fifty hours

        in your chain mail fist
        in your hot stone mouth
        in your implacable grasp
        held tight, my infant

i wept, i remembered
the slashing phallus
of a lover; i allowed
my body to be used
be a rippling pool of pain
because of you, o ghosts
o demons
a chamber of pain

        you are a chained male fist
        are a tongue and lips of stone
        you are a trap girding my hips
        who must be born
        for you are all wrapped up
        with my infant

o ghosts and demons
for twenty-five years
you held me at bay
you held me at bay
for twenty-five years

        with your hard and angry fist
        with your grinding teeth of stone
        with your clench upon my sex
        i fought you hard
        tore at myself to escape you
        ripped into flesh

i dreamt i remembered
the first time i flew
from my body. i was dropped
in the chasm of post-partum days
with a sick man and a child
slowly learning to breath
suckle
defecate

i had to survive, so i
creased myself shut
banished the demon

ghost, fist, demon
holding the child
i am so disenchanted

i am so disenchanted
holding the child

                was i this young
                or how old, the first time
                you slammed into me
                fist
                o fist fist
                fist that split me in two
                and remains
                embedded
                always a threat
                holding me firmly in pieces

i am after you now
with a body, two bodies

one you leaped out of
another, my own

i will struggle
you down

wrench back
what is mine

i will
name you

Before writing poems like this, I wrote poems that were hopelessly abstract and inscrutable. A great separation had developed between my bodymind and the hyper-intellectual fragment of mind I identified with, calling into question the term "individual." My life became a battleground for the two opposed aspects of myself. What empowered me as a writer and what has empowered my writings has been allowing a collapsing of that opposition, and a re-knitting of my person into a more unified whole.

Finding a voice as a writer means simply finding a way to let our stories out, to uncurl the muscles that are holding them stopped in our bodies. What is wise in this world exists equally inside of us and outside of us, and it is through collaboration that wisdom, stories, songs are made manifest.

To anyone hesitating on the brink of writing, I say, fall to it. To all of you who hear your own voice and say, boring, too familiar, not good enough, I say, of course your own voice is familiar, it is you. Sit closer to the audience, listen to what others have to say. To all of us who participate in writing and reading, in listening and speaking and listening again, I say thank you: it is an honour and a pleasure to participate in this world with you.

Let's close with a story.

Each time I sit down to set down a few words on this topic, I find myself walking, in fantasy, along a path that winds through the rainforest on the west coast of Canada.

Running beside this path under the trees is a creekbed of pale granitic stones, small and innumerable. Between these stones there weaves a flow of fresh, cold water, down from some mountainous beginning, rushing for the lowlands.

As I walk, something attracts me to the creekbed.

I leave the path and hunker down in a half-squat, among the stones.

Whatever it is that called to me is found. I pick it up, and hold it in my two hands.

NOTES

1 Presentation, "Finding a Voice as a Writer" panel, Women Writers' Weekend, Sydney, Australia, 6 August 1994.
2 "We are all soft bodies," a passing comment made by American crime writer Nikki Baker during the "Imagining Murder and Menace" panel at the Sixth International Feminist Book Fair, Melbourne, Australia, 29 July 1994.
3 *Wiles of Girlhood* (Vancouver: Press Gang Publishers, 1991).
4 Ibid.

Ahoy, Métis!

She says, "What did the captain say to the Half-breed sailor?"

I've dropped in for a visit with my sisters, who are renting rooms in a tired old building at the corner of Kingsway and Broadway, pending the owner's decision on what to do with it. It looks like a gas station, maybe a car lot, from the outside. From the inside the carpets are old and the walls are too white, but, well, it's alright.

I look at my sister and feel overwhelmingly bored, impatient. I think, *What has this got to do with me?* I think, *She's wasting my time.* I think, *She's looking pretty fragile.*

"I don't know," I finally respond. "What did the captain say?"

"Ahoy, Métis!!" she crows, nudging our younger sister. She laughs. Our sister looks embarrassed. I feel tense, angry. "We've been making up jokes to celebrate our Métis ancestry."

There is a wall of ice between us, thick with the urge to abandon, a gulf of hurt and distrust we have yet to begin to bridge. I am stiff, aloof. She is forcing jollity, forcing herself to trust. What she has said sounds so alien to me.

"Our what?"

A Trip in the Autumn

In the dim orange light he reached softly with a tattooed arm, brushed gently his squared fingertips in a light arc above and around her eye. It was closed, her eye, and swollen, purple brown in the orange light. Inside of him, almost behind him, a quiet voice was speaking monotonously, observing, recording and reporting without inflection facts, possibilities, choices.

I believe, he thought, *that I did this. I believe I did.*

The woman was curled protectively on the floor of the tent, eyes closed against the light and arms tucked close to her breast, bony hands pillowing her head. Her legs were folded below her torso, attempting in some way to re-create the scene to one of solitary warmth, security, well-being.

Blood coursed freely through her head, her neck and arms, breasts and shoulders. Blood and adrenalin flowed through her folded legs. Periodically a spasm clutched and released the great muscles in her calves and thighs, in her buttocks and belly, and her body wracked and jumped for quick brief seconds and was still.

The air in the tent was quiet and superficially peaceful, still as the slyly held breath of a reluctant victim, relaxed as the breath of a con artist who has already made the decision to kill, must now only wait, wait and be silent.

The voice rolled on inside him. It spoke of the passion she had raised up in him, the passion of fear and terror and anger, and how cold he'd become after spending his passion again and again. Open hand and closed fist, and voice, raised sharp and lowered grim. How his hands had curled so easily around her neck and squeezed and squeezed . . . He blinked. The voice rolled on, reporting the succession of looks in her eyes, first anger, fear, anger again, and then dim, unfocussed, rolling back in her head as her face and body gave over to a look of vacancy and absence.

He lay with one arm propping him up, one arm shyly reaching across the short distance of the tent, one finger touching her softly. His eyes, large and blue, roamed gently from feature to feature of her downturned, sad looking face. Her bruised and swelling eye, her nose with a touch of blood embroidering one nostril. Her neck curved into shadow, guarded by her hands, tucked between them for protection. His passion was spent and the coldness of mental precision was fading too. He felt the same softness and affection he felt every night, watching her sleep, and daily as her gaze moved along the horizon and then turned back to him, smiling, peaceful.

He watched and touched her face in the failing light of evening. His inner peace was punctuated by a tug or a twitch, a silent pressing sense from the depths, wordless cry, message of dumb urgency, fury of alarm. The fear again. The sense of danger.

"Does this bother you?" he asked and her body trembled, flinched at the sound. She shook her head slowly, a negative reply. Her eyes flickered open and then closed and she answered softly, "No."

He fought to maintain control of himself, of the situation so recently mastered, but the fear was at his throat again, forcing him to speak, pushing out words. "And what if I said I wanted sex?"

Inside she quailed, her being shook. Her wide awake mind flicked lightly over the whole situation. She spoke.

"No, no, I don't want to because . . . my feeling is neutral right now. If there's time, I might come to . . . want to . . ."

How gratifying. Proof gathered from the outside world, evidence to smother the inborn terror. In time, ignoring the fearful being, brushing under conscious perception the separated voice which rolled and rolled, he asked, "Do you love me?"

When she affirmed, a character spoke through his mouth, sternly requesting, "The truth?"

She replied, "Yes."

Once again his body became easy. He felt safe, safe as a baby. All through the night a restless, angrier phantom peered through his sleep, and watched and watched his hostage.

Come morning he ordered her to take the canteen to the nearby river and fill it. While she was gone he packed up the tent. The shoes and the soiled trousers at the base of the tree were reminders, making him nervous and tense. Seconds ticked by and there was something moving at a high speed, jarring inside him. Some movement obsessively slapped like a windshield wiper again and again. Though he breathed and tried to slow his body down, he was forced upright and a little too quickly, too stiffly, followed her path through the bush.

Halfway to the river he came to a clearing. She appeared, far to the left near the highway, walking across the grass toward him. Sheepish, trusting again but jittery, he presented her with a packet of sugar. A gift.

She carried the water.

Up on the highway again, they were walking. The rain sluiced down frosty and it was cold, quieter than usual. She didn't seem afraid. At times she appeared to diminish, and at times to loom high above and overhead, frighteningly large. She answered his questions and comments politely, made inane comments, but mostly she chose to be silent. She walked.

His heart was pounding. A terrible cinch had been applied about his chest, and it just kept pulling, tight, tight. The rain and the cold were discomfort, the damp penetrating the old injured knee and starting an ache, a throb. His belly was foul with hunger. The rhythm of stepping, of walking, was lulling. Inside the voice was barely audible, droning. The fear and the love, distrust and terror, discomfort and lack of a plan all gelled together while he walked and he wallowed, faraway, dulling.

She walked behind him.

She opened her mind in the safety of not being watched. One thought, one and then another coming together, tracing event to event and opening up into feeling. Terror, horror, revulsion and anger, pride and horror and anger. Then in a calm cool voice within she said, *No, calm now, time for this later, be cool. Be calm and be cool.* She checked out her body, surprised that in most places she felt fine. Neck very stiff and sore, a bruised knee, the flesh of her face very tender and distorted. Odd, unnatural. She began inside an incantation, hate songs for the man whose step was ragged before her.

Murderer. Murderer! she thought and breaking into a silent scream, *You fucking bastard,* rode on the wave of that and got off. She breathed to calm her body. She repeated words in her mind to keep the information fixed, firm. *He tried to kill me. He wants to enslave me. I may yet die. I may get a chance to kill him. What I must do is bide my time, watch for a chance for definitive action, a clean break or a very quick death but no fuck ups, nothing part way.* As she walked she formulated words, ideas. Slowly her mind retreated from shock, the shocked numb state that had followed the absolute awareness that had lasted until the immediate danger of dying had passed.

The rain poured heavily down, freezing and mingling with snowflakes and filling the air with a pale whitish grey for miles. The highway they tread trickled down the temple of the flat Albertan north, winter creeping quickly toward them. Finally a small truck stopped, a wan driver offered them a ride. They climbed into the vehicle and, in time, became warm.

A truckstop appeared at the roadside. They pulled in, the two men silently leaving the truck to pick up some coffee. She unrolled a window and peered at herself in the sideview, startled to find her eye the colour of blood. Quickly she shut the window, daunted by the sight. The men approached through the rain across the parking lot.

The driver put on some taped music, "To help you relax," he said. The music was soothing. As she listened to the hypnotic Christian lyrics, glorying in dependence, in suffering, she began to feel angry again, angry and sick.

All the long day was the same, the droning of engines, drumming of rain, miles unrolling so steady and hours as steadily passing, passing. He was touched for a long while with feeling foolish, and tried to look on the funny side of the situation. She refused to join in. No longer feeling the competent hero, the bloodless killer, he looked at her with round awkward eyes, winced at the marks of his destruction and turned away. His precarious sense of self was shifting. He was suffering a loss of faith and losing his direction. *Go south, go south,* a voice chanted inside. He looked at her and felt scared. Her eyes so sad and serious held some message, some intelligence coming through he was unable to decipher.

He said, "You look so serious when I tell you I love you." She just looked at him, her mouth closed. Then he felt stupid.

On the second day they were walking on the highway route heading south, through a great long city. The farms were gone, and the trees. The first signs of settlement gave way quickly to car lots and then to an ocean of houses. He chose a path that took them through its midst. After their time in the bush the two city dwellers were disoriented, alien. They stopped at a small café for coffee. Dismal. She was tense. He was self-absorbed and his mood, plummeting.

He talked of going to the eastern States, where his grandparents had a cottage. He'd lived there as a boy, which was a long time ago. Or maybe it was a movie he'd seen. She listened and, in time, began to encourage such thoughts, observing how unrealistic he was, how he allowed himself to believe in such slender chances.

She told him she was very reluctant to leave the country, "Canada is my home."

They walked in silence some more, past stores and houses and a steady stream of cars. They found a quiet place to pause, a flight of wooden steps at the edge of a park, sat down and lit cigarettes.

"It's unfair," she said softly. She moved carefully. Whatever she knew of this strange man, he was not totally stupid. He'd slipped from familiar kindness before, when she'd made a move toward leaving. He saw himself as a loner, lawless, with nothing to lose but her, her presence in his life, her life. She saw herself as a young woman who had made a big mistake, talking to strangers.

"The reason I want to go there," he said, "the reason I want to go now is that the place there feels safe to me." After a few moments, he offered another reason. "I'm running scared. I don't know of what but I am, there it is."

She would take another risk, a small one, walk a little more closely to who she really was, her real feelings. She began with words of compassion, "I can see why you're frightened." She said, "It seems like your life has suffered a few turn arounds lately . . ."

"Turn around nothing," he snapped, his voice stronger. "It was shattered. All I had before was myself and my work, that was enough. Now, I can't believe in my work anymore, and—I can't, believe in myself anymore, either . . ."

Long moments of silence, as she knew very well what he meant.

They walked again.

He felt a little better, eased, at least the confusion wasn't rolling in on top of itself anymore. With talking, at least he didn't have to be so self-contained. Trusting. Opening up to a friend who yesterday was a hostage, the day before, a victim, the day before that, what—a girl, a woman.

She, too, fell to trusting. Sensing the situation was almost in hand, she pushed herself to take some action. They were nearing the edge of the city again. It was now or the long risky wait until the next city. *He trusts,* she thought, *his defenses are down. It's not perfect, but the chances may never be better.*

She opened her mouth.

Softly but firmly she spoke, with the steel edge of immovable will gleaming through her words. "I know you trust me . . . but . . . I . . . want the control of my life back, in my own hands."

With the revelation came a surge of energy, her entrails shook as she cast away the cover of lies.

Swept with agitation, his pace quickened. She kept stride, feeling the ripples of nervous convulsing shaking the power out of her muscles, adrenaline surging in, confusing her senses. Each walked, head held high against separate waves of terror, each one almost overwhelmed with the size of the struggle.

She fell a pace behind him. *Act now,* she hissed to herself.

Like an animal, a mad horse or a bear she went into the street, dodging the traffic. With a squeal he came after her. Crowing in a faraway voice, he was quickly upon her.

"You're gonna get killed," he shrieked.

"That is the point, you asshole—"

He dragged her back to the side of the road. She sat down on the sidewalk. Kneeling before her with hands on her shoulders he begged. Something like a foggy sail rose up inside him. He screeched at her, trying to soothe. "I'm not gonna hurt you. I don't want to hurt you . . ."

Mind and body confused by too much adrenaline, by too much or not enough action, there was no more reason to hold on, to calm down. She recognized rage, and she sputtered, "What difference does it make *how* you take my life?"

A car drew up. A tall man in a leisure suit hunched over the steering wheel. A frightened blonde woman with a baby on her knee sat beside him. The scene slowly unwound as the people in the car asked her, once, twice, "Do you need help? Do you want a ride?"

She nodded dumbly, yes, and the man came out of the car and moved toward her. The car door was opened. She climbed in.

At her companion's request, she lowered the car window an inch. Instead of the promised words, he thrust his fingers in, gripping the glass. Their faces met across the pane. Something hard and final happened to her, inside her, as she looked into his eyes and saw, though they stared right back at her, how empty they were. How disconnected.

He had to be first peeled off the side, then out from under the car, disentangled. She watched him. He was high on his own sense of drama. A single line repeated to excess, "Don't go don't go don't go don't go . . ."

They drove off.

He threw a clump of dirt after the car.

Losing Angel

Angel was my best friend. We lived a few blocks apart. We went to the same school. My family had just moved in from the prairie and her family had lived here on the west coast since time immemorial. We leaned together and talked and laughed, we played in her front yard, we shared things.

One day Angel had a brilliant idea. Instead of hanging out at her house as usual, we went a few blocks further, went into a shop and came out again with a small pouch of powdered hot chocolate.

"You don't need money?"

"You just walk in and take it."

"Cool."

We weren't greedy. On our excursions we only picked out a few things we could enjoy on the way home. We spread out our business, so nobody got mad at us.

I don't know how they ever found out. Maybe we did get greedy one time, some adult found a stash and told all the others. But find out they did, not just one or two, but everybody at once.

I was not allowed to play with my best friend, Angel. Her grown-up sister, like a mother, yelled at me to go home when

I came to visit. I was lectured by my mother, my father, my teacher, and in a very forbidding scene, by the old school principal. He sat at his desk, avuncular, hands folded. The huge, grim, brush-cut vice-principal stood behind him, hands behind his back, staring at me, his endless frown laced with traces of menace. I was brought to the Safeway one evening, and forced to both confess and apologize to the store manager. I was overwhelmed by it all, I trembled and sobbed. All he asked was that I not do it again. I promised that I would not do it again so he gave me a copy of the Christmas flyer.

It had pictures of Angels on it, not the ordinary Angel who I couldn't see any more, but long faceless creatures arcing away from the words on the page, with harps and horns and wings and white dresses.

Last Year's Corpse

We walk back to the co-operative from the end-of-the-line bus stop and coffee house, my son, who is four, and myself, twenty-nine. Although he wasn't born at the co-operative, my son has celebrated each of his birthdays here, and soon his sibling will arrive to do the same. His father and I, caught between the economic derision of parents and the desire to perpetuate life on earth, joined the co-operative as soon as we found it. It offered us shelter in a hostile world.

Within the co-operative, we have moved twice, from building to building. This day, my son has decided we should follow the route we used to take when we lived in the reno-vated warehouse, cutting through that building and the courtyard to get to our current apartment, instead of the usual and more direct route. Because the day is sunny and I have a little patience for a change, I agree. I follow his lead.

As we pass the alley that is stopped by the courtyard gates, we see Daedalus breaking up the mostly dismantled remains of somebody's furniture. My son turns on his heel and bolts down the alley toward him.

"Hey, Dade! What are you doing?!"

Dade looks up and smiles, forehead crinkling. "Hello, Stu. What are *you* doing?"

Dade drops a long-handled tool to the gravel and begins collecting the broken bits of wood and metal scattered on the ground around him. He tosses them a few at a time into a huge orange garbage container.

"I was at daycare. What's that?"

My son's face is like the sky, open, clear, receptive.

"This? I was just breaking up some old furniture. Don't touch this, now." He indicates a board with nails thrusting out every few inches. He raises his voice to address me. "Yeah, they were cleaning out the daycare downstairs, lots of old junk left in there. Got to break it up so they can take it away."

I nod. He's talking about the co-op women, the unused daycare space, the garbage men.

Daedalus is an ex-logger. Like so many around here, he kept at it until his health had been so compromised he had no other option but to quit. Ten years away from that bush-city-bush cycle, and the wild alcoholism that often goes with it, he doesn't look in the least frail. He's a primary volunteer at the co-op and he works as my partner's boss elsewhere in this dense neighbourhood.

Every year at Christmas time, Dade gives all the children at the co-op chocolate Santas. In the summer he works in the garden, waiting for the children to find him and bait him, then turning on them with the water hose, eliciting joyous screams and breathless giggles.

"Hey, Dade." Stuart moves right up beside him, the

crown of his small head parallel to the top of Dade's hip-bone. Stuart is respectfully examining three long-handled tools that lie on the gravel. One looks like a wrench, another resembles a pair of scissors, the third is definitely a crowbar. "What are these for?"

Dade bends down over the tools and picks up the crow-bar. He looks directly into Stuart's wide brown eyes.

"This is to knock your mom on the head," he tells him, showing him the tool. I am shocked.

"This," he says, picking up the shears, "is to cut her up in little pieces." I begin to feel sick. I glance around. We are standing in the alley on a bright sunny day. The garbage container beside us is right outside the garbage chute, where three floors up a woman was found murdered, just a year ago.

"And this," Dade declares, flourishing the final tool before my son's very serious face, "is to pick up the pieces and throw them in the garbage."

We stand in silence. Dade straightens up and laughs. He throws a final shard into the dumpster. My son looks at me. I bow my head.

"That," I say, "was disgusting."

We cut through the building beside us, my son runs and I walk the length of it, emerging into the courtyard. We traverse the courtyard, along concrete pathways through grass, flower-ing bushes, children playing. The courtyard is a renowned oasis in the inner city, even strangers stop to breath in the freshness through the grid fence. We climb a skeletal staircase, I pull out my keys and open the outside door.

Stuart runs into the hall and throws himself against our

apartment door. He grins at me, delighted to find the door opens.

"Daddy!"

Stuart tumbles into the apartment. I follow. We see his father smiling over the half-wall that divides kitchen from living room. Clattering dishes in the sink, steam rising from the stove behind him.

"Daddy," Stuart shouts, "we saw Dade!"

"You did?!"

"Yeah!"

"Yeah," I say, with a rush of feeling. "Dade is an *asshole*."

Stuart spins and looks at me, shocked. Brian looks at me too, and asks, "What happened?"

"Stuart asked him for some simple information." Sounds like I'm shouting. I don't care if I'm shouting. I go on. *"Instead of just telling him what they're for, he gives him all this stupid fucking bull-shit. Stuart wanted to know what his tools were for and instead of just telling him what they're for he said,"* sounds to me like I'm scared, *"they're for chopping me up and throwing me,"* yeah, definitely I'm scared, *"into the garbage!"*

Stuart is sobbing. Brian looks horrified. I'm shaking like a small leaf in a big wind.

Although several people knew the body was there, it was Dade who found her, Dade who, instead of leaving the blocked door unexamined, responded appropriately, investigated. He found the young woman's body, called security, the board of directors, called the police.

"What a stupid way to talk to a little kid, or at all!"

Especially to a young mother who won't let her son watch TV or play with guns, who wants her son to know everything worth knowing and feels that what she has to pass on is sparse, fragmented. "Especially to a little boy who just wants to know what the tools are for." Especially to a little girl who was methodically trained to stay away from strangers, to ignore the crimes seen around her, to shut up completely and to never, never ask questions. "I hate Dade. I hate that asshole."

Stuart is screaming and sobbing. Brian is standing in front of me, jarred, helpless. The little boy cries from across the room, "But we *like* Dade!"

I can see that woman, ill-treated guest, rushing from apartment to apartment, hear her pounding on doors, desperately seeking assistance. I imagine my neighbour, stirred by her knock, watching through the peephole as the two young men who were about to beat her to death entered from the stairwell. See him pull back from the door, shakily push papers around his apartment, looking for the security phone number, not finding it.

She was found the following morning in the garbage room, in her underwear.

"Dade can be very nice," I admit. "But I am very, very angry with him right now."

"Well," Stuart responds, "you should *tell* him."

Not that I could feel any of this, standing out there in the alley, or walking the distance from that place to this. Not that I felt anything more than shock and shame, until I walked into the apartment and was greeted by my partner's smiling, safe face.

"Yes, yes, you're right. I know I should."

Brian hugs me. I stand with him for a moment and then pull away. I find myself slipping back in time, living alone in a rented room, starting up out of my bed at a scream of utmost terror, very near. I pace the tiny room. I look out the little window I'd left open for a cool summer breeze. All I can see in this now silent evening, that might be a clue to what I've heard, is another open window, in the apartment building next door. I have no phone. Nobody in the neighbourhood calls or stirs. There are no sirens.

I'm back, with Stuart, with Brian. I slip into the arms of an old rocking chair my grandmother gave me, years ago. I have rocked in this chair from time to time, on special occasions, all through my life. My son clambers onto my lap. He holds onto my neck until his last sobs have passed. His body relaxes into mine.

"I love you, Mom."

"I love you too, Stuart."

"Supper is almost ready," Brian says, appealing.

Now I'm fifteen years old and my red-headed neighbour is smiling. She is inviting me to go to court with her, something she must do for her high school project. Now I'm listening to the coroner's stiff language and watching his expressionless face. Now I'm listening to a guy close to my age, describing an escalating day and night, where a girl agrees to share a few drinks, how the guys get to tormenting her, how everybody there gets a blow job, everybody gets to gang rape, everybody takes a hand in her murder. How they chop her up, how they toss all of her parts in a muddy field.

Now I hear Brian's voice. "Want to talk some more?"

I never talked to that red-headed girl anymore, after that. She avoided me. Not 'til she was moving away did I see her smile again.

Now I'm smelling my son's hair.

"Not right now," I murmur, burrowing my face in the warm small person before me. Then, a minute later, "It was right by the garbage chute, where he said that."

"Upsetting," he says, an acknowledgement.

"Yeah!" Stuart turns, joining in. "He was breaking up furniture!" The boy scrambles off my lap and runs into the kitchen, grabbing Brian around his legs. "Can I have a drink?"

I look around the room that is full of my things and my partner's things, our books and furniture, our packs, Stuart's toys and artwork. Rocking in my grandmother's chair, I imagine talking to Daedalus. I look into his ordinary face.

I'm trying to raise my son well, and . . .

My son needs information about the world, and it's up to you and I . . .

Dade, I'm disappointed with you . . .

Dade, that was inappropriate . . .

You hurt my feelings.

You scared me.

Why did you say that?

I think about talking to Daedalus and practising what I preach. But I can't imagine talking to him like this.

Breasting the Waves

When I first saw her she was on a bench in an alley, quite a nice alley, bright with the midday sun. She was leaning way over, putting a big empty wine bottle into the long grass under the bench. At that point, as she was lifting her head, I was guessing that when her brilliant black hair moved aside I would see that she was a woman, and that she was very sick with the booze. I guess I was right, at least I could see it all there, in her face.

When I saw her next, a few minutes later, we were at the bus stop, my white boyfriend, our new baby and me. She came up and waved her hand. *Lady, lady hey,* she said. She didn't come too close, didn't want to scare me maybe, or maybe she was held off by the white boyfriend. She couldn't get her mouth to speak to me. *Wait a minute, wait,* she said, and she pulled her shirt very high, showing me her breast.

When I saw her beautiful breast, there on the avenue, dancing below her sad face, her long shining hair, I didn't know what to do. I didn't know why she wanted me to look at her breast.

Three men walked up and said *hey* to her. She leaned close onto one of them, tried to explain. I heard just the bare edges of her words, enough to figure out that she was offering or asking or talking about nursing the baby.

I gave one of her friends my cigarette. I admired the carving his brother was doing. As we spoke, I wanted to turn and ask, *hey lady, what's going on, what can I do to help you right now?* But the booze held me off. I just hung onto that new baby, wrapped in a blanket close to my breast. She said good-bye to the guy she knew.

Turning to go, she lost her balance and fell, landing hard against a storefront and the grey sidewalk. The guys helped her up. She looked wicked at the friend she'd been talking to, as if he'd done it to her. She was really angry. They helped her to the bench.

One guy said to me, *pretty sad, eh, but I guess that's life.*

So many words and feelings crowded through, I just looked at the woman, at the guy, at the carving, at the cars passing by and the big bus coming. I looked at the guy who was standing by me and I . . .

. . . came to the healing circle. Thought it would be women only, and was wrong.

About the Author

Four kids. Four books.

A writer, mother, and counsellor/activist, Joanne Arnott is of Métis/mixed Native and European ancestry. She studied English at the University of Windsor, Ontario, and began publishing after attending WestWord, with Beth Brant. She was born in Winnipeg, in 1960. A double Sagittarian with Virgo rising, "the rugged Ms. Arnott" (*Globe & Mail*) has made her home on the west coast for over a decade. Her first book, *Wiles of Girlhood* (Press Gang Publishers, 1991) won the Canadian League of Poets' Gerald Lampert Award for best first book of poetry. This was followed by *My Grass Cradle* (Press Gang Publishers, 1992), poetry, and *Ma Mac-Donald* (Women's Press, 1993), a book on natural childbirth for children, playfully illustrated by Mary Anne Barkhouse.

After seven years of co-facilitating Unlearning Racism workshops and ten years of peer counselling, Joanne has begun drawing on this background to facilitate writing workshops that are inclusive and often issue-oriented. She has done readings and presented workshops in Canada and Australia, for a variety of groups and organizations. Current writing projects include a poetry manuscript, *Spiders & Dogs*, and *Country-Born*, an anthology of writing by Métis and other mixed race (Native/non-Native) authors. People interested in contributing to the *Country-Born* anthology and/or having Joanne come to your community, please contact her c/o Press Gang Publishers.

Press Gang Publishers has been producing vital and
provocative books by women since 1975.

A free catalogue of our books in print is available from
Press Gang Publishers, 101-225 East 17TH Avenue,
Vancouver, B.C. V5V 1A6 Canada